HER COWBOY BLIND DATE

EASTER IN GILEAD

NARELLE ATKINS

Her Cowboy Blind Date

1st edition 2023 — Narelle Atkins

Narelle Atkins

PO BOX 512

Jamison Centre ACT 2614

AUSTRALIA

www.narelleatkins.com

Cover Art by Jess Mastorakos

Her Cowboy Blind Date/Narelle Atkins. —1st ed.

ISBN: 1-922915-07-6

ISBN-13: 978-1-922915-07-8

❀ Created with Vellum

CHAPTER 1

Bek Montford closed the glass door to the dental office and wished she could stop the throbbing pain in her mouth. The painkillers had worn off, and her gums were numb and sore from the poking and prodding to fix her problem molar. She hated going to the dentist, hated having her teeth cleaned and polished, and hated having to endure the drilling and filling to fix her tooth.

She walked to the elevator bay near the level three suite and pressed the down button. All she wanted to do was return to her campus dorm room at Gilead Bible College, crawl into bed, and rest until the discomfort in her mouth eased. Thankfully, she didn't have any Tuesday afternoon classes this week.

A tall man carrying a beige cowboy hat approached the elevator from the other direction.

Bek nodded, acknowledging his smile with what she hoped was a polite smile of her own. She swung her gaze back to the closed elevator doors, unable to feel the left side of her face.

At least she'd avoided another awkward introduction with friendly Gilead townsfolk where she needed to remember to call herself Becky. She'd left Bek Montford — and the mistakes she'd made during the last few years — on the other side of the world. Gilead was a fresh start, beginning with a switch to her childhood nickname.

Bek had been in Kansas for five months and no longer gawked at the real-life cowboys she came across in the small college town. Cowboys didn't mosey down the street in the Sydney beachside suburb where she'd grown up in Australia.

The elevator pinged, the doors opened, and the blond cowboy, who looked around her age, indicated for her to enter the empty space first. She stepped inside, appreciating his manners. Maybe at twenty-two she was too young to be old-fashioned, but she liked gallant men who treated women like ladies. Unlike her Aussie ex-boyfriend, who wouldn't recognize integrity if it slapped him in the face.

They began their descent and the level two number flashed. Bang. A grinding noise, followed by a drop of a few feet, brought them to a halt in between floors.

Bek's stomach sunk in tandem with the sharp elevator drop. They were stuck. She couldn't feel half of her face. Her jaw had hurt when she'd tried to talk with the receptionist and pay her dental bill. Her mouth and her hip pocket had taken a hit, and she couldn't continue to ignore the cowboy stranded with her.

She looked up at the cowboy. Steel-capped work boots, denim jeans, button-up shirt under his jacket, and a clean-shaven jaw. His short blond hair, strong and lean physique, and sun-kissed complexion in the middle of winter suggested he worked outdoors. His eyebrows were pulled together, his concern for their situation evident.

His calm ocean-blue eyes locked on her, drawing her in and taking charge. "I'll press the call button."

She nodded, dragging her gaze away from his beautiful eyes and handsome face. He smelled good, with not even a whiff of sweat or farm animal scent in their confined space. Six people in this elevator would be a tight fit. She stepped back toward a wall, putting an extra two feet of space between them.

The dial tone echoing through the elevator microphone droned on and on. Why hadn't they picked up the call?

The cowboy pressed the button again, and this time a man answered. Twenty minutes was the wait time for a maintenance person to arrive and manually lower the elevator by six feet to the level one entrance on Main Street.

Bek leaned back against the elevator wall and closed her eyes for a few seconds, thankful she'd soon be out of the claustrophobic space. She looked forward to the short walk to her dorm in the crisp January weather. The lightheadedness from the meds added to her fatigue.

"Looks like we're stuck here for a while," the cowboy said.

She nodded and pulled her phone out of her jeans pocket. She may not be able to talk, but she could type a note on her phone.

Been to dentist, can't talk. Not first time stuck in elevator. We'll be out soon.

Bek passed her phone to the cowboy and he read her note.

He studied her, his mouth tilting into a half smile. "That explains why you aren't panicking."

She reached for her phone, avoiding contact with his fingertips, and typed her reply before passing it back to him.

Stuck in a hotel elevator by myself between levels 17 and 18, no one answered call button. Called hotel on my phone. They lowered elevator to lobby.

He read her words on the phone screen and handed it back. "That's why you're not worried about a six-foot drop."

Bek nodded, liking the soothing drawl in his deep voice. He wasn't stressed and had kept a cool head in a sticky situation. There was no tan line on his ring finger. He must be in a relationship because he was too good-looking to be single. Not that she should care about his relationship status. She wasn't looking for a relationship, and especially not with a cute cowboy she'd randomly met in an elevator.

She glanced around, spotting a laminated passion play advertisement stuck on the back wall beside her. The Gilead passion play preparations were in full swing, and she'd earn credits for her Biblical history study program by volunteering to join the crew. Auditions for the actors started tomorrow. The annual event prior to Easter was a tourist attraction that drew visitors to Gilead from all over the country.

"Will you be seeing the play?" he asked.

She nodded, feeling like a dodo bird, but she didn't tap a reply on her phone. He didn't need to know her level of involvement in the play.

The cowboy smiled and her tummy did a little back flip. Ugh. It must be the tight quarters situation combined with the meds that had her hormones hopping like a jumping jack. She was too aware of him, standing only three feet away, for her own good. The last time she'd allowed herself to be charmed by a good-looking stranger had ended in disaster.

"Do you mind if I do stuff on my phone?" His kind eyes expressed his concern. "Since you can't talk and all."

She attempted a smile, typed a new note, and passed him her phone.

All good, tooth pain isn't fun. Thanks for understanding.

He read her message. "Sorry about your tooth. Did they give you any painkillers?"

She nodded and gave him a thumbs up.

"Hope you feel better soon." He placed her phone in the palm of her hand, his fingertips lightly touching her bare wrist.

Tingles of awareness shot through her and she gripped the phone, worried she'd embarrass herself by dropping it. His striking blue eyes radiated a warmth that pulled her in, an attraction that was appealing and dangerous in equal measure. He was a charming stranger, and she wasn't going to be fooled again by a beguiling smile and sweet words.

She redirected her attention to her phone. Of course, she'd gone dark on social media and deleted the apps. She'd left her ear buds in her dorm, and there was nothing compelling to do on her phone to distract her from the cowboy. She'd read and replied to all her messages from family back home while waiting to see the dentist.

Don't look at him, don't engage him in conversation, and don't reveal any personal information. The best way to avoid attention and stay under the radar in a small Midwestern town. The safest path to avoid getting her heart broken.

Sam Williams pulled his gaze away from the pretty lady stranded with him in the elevator and sent apology messages to his boss and next customer. He should be leaving now for his afternoon job at a ranch out of town. So much for attempting a discreet visit to his lawyer's office during his lunch break to sign the paperwork and claim his inheritance. He was now the proud part owner of the Colorado family ranch that had been in his mother's family for generations.

A new message flashed on his phone. Sam was thankful he had an understanding boss. His track record for punctuality had helped. At least he'd squeezed in a burger for lunch after cleaning up for the lawyer meeting. He'd spent part of his morning fixing a tractor that had broken down in a muddy field.

Sam should have taken the stairs. He would have walked down two flights if an old knee injury from his high school football days hadn't started acting up at Christmas. He'd put off making an appointment with a physical therapist, figuring the cold weather was the problem, and the reason he'd felt twinges this morning. If he'd taken the stairs, he wouldn't be stuck in an elevator with a dark-haired beauty who was doing her best to ignore him.

Her straight hair had fallen forward over her face, her attention focused on the phone screen in her hand. He guessed she was a college student, although the expensive woolen coat draped over her arm suggested she wasn't short of money. She wore a plain long sleeve t-shirt, ripped jeans, and black lace-up Doc Martens boots. He didn't understand the ripped-jeans-in-winter trend that his cousin, Cindy, insisted was the universal college student uniform.

The Gilead population swelled during the college semesters with an influx of students from around the country. His elevator companion looked like she belonged in a city, but without hearing her accent he couldn't discern if she was East Coast, West Coast, or somewhere in between.

Minutes ticked by and he replied to Mom's message, confirming he'd signed his inheritance paperwork.

He snuck a glance at the girl leaning back against the elevator wall. Brows drawn together, eyes closed, and mouth pulled in a tight line. She was in pain and he couldn't think of a way to ease her discomfort. He didn't even know her name.

He shook his head. Their lack of communication was for the best. He hadn't imagined the spark when he'd given back her phone, and her wide-eyed reaction had suggested the feeling was mutual. He respected her decision to zone him out and not play the flirty games his ex-girlfriend had excelled in. Miley strung him along for years, only to dump him a few short months before marrying Sam's best friend's brother.

Which had dumped Sam in his current wedding guest dilemma. Pete was getting married at Easter, and Sam didn't have a plus-one lined up for the wedding. Cindy was pushing him to get back on the dating horse, and his cousin wanted to set him up on a blind date. He didn't know if he was prepared to deal with the inevitable dating and relationship drama.

Noise sounded from below his feet, and the elevator moved lower, inch by inch.

Pretty girl looked up, her long dark lashes framing her distinctive sky-blue eyes. Her cute smile was still a bit lopsided, a side effect from the dental procedure. For her sake, he hoped and prayed she'd arrive home before her tooth pain became unbearable.

"We'll be out of here in a few minutes," he said.

She gave him a thumbs up and slipped her phone back into her jeans pocket. He got the message loud and clear, and he stayed quiet until the elevator doors opened on level one.

A middle-aged maintenance guy smiled. "You folks doing okay?"

"We're fine," Sam said, standing back to allow pretty girl to exit first. "Thanks for rescuing us."

Pretty girl nodded and waved goodbye, then took off, high-tailing it out of the elevator as if she was escaping a burning building.

The maintenance guy shook his head. "If you're going to get stuck in an elevator, then being stranded with a girl like her isn't a bad deal. Did you catch her name? Or get her number?"

Sam chuckled. "She'd just been to the dentist and couldn't talk."

"That's a shame." He shook his head again, this time more slowly. "A missed opportunity, if you ask me. I met my wife by accident at a car wash almost twenty years ago. I helped her polish her car, and the rest is history." His grin beamed his happily married status.

Sam stepped out of the elevator and shook the man's hand. "Good for you, and I'm glad you got the girl."

"Too right. Sometimes it can be those split-second decisions that can change your life. What if I hadn't washed my car that day?"

Sam nodded. "A good thing you did. Thanks again, and have a

good day." He waved goodbye to the maintenance guy and headed for the door. His truck was parked a few blocks up the street, and he welcomed the fresh air after being trapped indoors.

His phone rang and he glanced at the screen. Cindy. He'd better take the call or she'd be calling him back all afternoon.

"Hey, Sam." Cindy's bright greeting boomed in his ear. "How's your day been?"

"Good, but I'm running late for my next job." He headed along the sidewalk, waving to the people he knew along the way. Talking to Cindy would help him reach his truck faster than having to stop and talk to half the town.

"That doesn't sound like you. What happened?"

"Nothing much." He refused to tell his cousin about the pretty girl in the elevator, adding more fuel to Cindy's matchmaking ideas. Pretty girl was probably in a relationship. He should forget he met her. That would be the sensible way to handle their brief encounter. If only he was feeling sensible.

"You still there?" Cindy asked.

"Yeah, I'm crossing Main Street a block from my truck. Is there a reason you're calling?"

"There is a reason." Cindy coughed and cleared her throat. "Have you given any more thought to my blind date suggestion?"

"Seriously, Cindy. Can you let it go?"

"No, I can't. You have that wedding to attend on Easter Saturday. Miley will be there with Matt — her new husband."

Her words were jarring and headache inducing. He'd been out of town with Dad's family for Thanksgiving weekend when Matt and Miley had tied the knot.

"Sam, are you listening to me? You can't avoid Miley now she's Pete's sister-in-law."

"Yeah." Sam let out a long breath, and sucked in another deep breath, quickening his pace. He didn't need to be reminded over and over that his high school sweetheart had married Pete's older brother. Sam had tried to decline Pete's invitation to be a groomsman. Tried and failed. He hoped Pete would listen and understand why it would be awkward.

"Sam, are you ignoring me?"

"Calm down." Cindy's harping was worse than Mom's, who'd dropped a few dozen hints on his need for a wife and Mom's need for grandbabies during their Christmas and New Year break at the ranch. The downside of being an only child — all the pressure for grandchildren fell on his shoulders. Between Mom, Cindy, and his aunt, he'd been relieved to end his twenty-fifth birthday family celebrations and drive home to Gilead, alone. "Pete and Emma's wedding is three months away —"

"And that time will fly by fast and you won't have a date for the wedding."

"Cindy, it's not going to happen. I'll go to the wedding by myself. It'll be fine."

"Nothing about this situation is fine. A girl on your arm at that wedding will stop the tongues wagging and smooth over the situation. You'll show the world you've moved on, and everyone will be happy."

Everyone except Sam. He couldn't start dating any of the single girls at church in good conscience, knowing he was moving to the ranch. His new plan to either transfer to a new job in Colorado or set up his own farm mechanic business would mean working away from the ranch for long stretches of time. A wife didn't figure in his plans. "This mythical girl you keep talking about isn't going to suddenly turn up in Gilead at the right time. I think you're dreaming."

"I know you're wrong because I've found the girl."

"What? You're joking, right?"

"No. I've been sounding her out and I think she's perfect for you."

"I don't want to get married —"

"Who's talking about getting married? She's our age, and she's smart and attractive and fun to be around."

He reached his truck and beeped it open. "If that's true, then why isn't she in a relationship? She sounds too good to be true."

"She's a city girl from Sydney, Australia, and she has a fabulous accent. And I know you love listening to Aussies talk."

That was a truth he couldn't deny. "What's an Aussie girl like her doing in small-town Kansas?"

"Studying at Gilead Bible College with me. She's in my dorm, and we've become good friends."

He opened the door of his truck. "Good for you, Cindy. This is a bad idea —"

"No, it's not, because she's just like you."

"Really? Is that so?" He sat in the driver's seat and closed the door. When was Cindy going to admit defeat and give up by closing the door on this ridiculous idea?

"Like you, she's been burned and isn't looking for anything serious. She'll graduate with her Biblical studies diploma in May and fly home to her old life in Australia."

"This is all pie in the sky." He rolled down the window in his truck. "Why would she want to go on a blind date with me?"

"You're both Christians, for starters. And you might surprise yourself by wanting to be her friend. You may even like spending time with her."

"Hold on a minute. I'm in the truck and switching to hands-free." He turned over the engine and rubbed his fist over his eyes. Cindy wasn't going to let up. He thought about the car wash story, and the split-second decisions that could change a person's life.

"Okay, Cindy." He pulled out of the parking space.

"Are you saying yes?"

"I'm saying yes. Will you get off my case and let me get back to work?"

Cindy squealed, and he turned down the truck volume, glad his phone wasn't close to his ear.

"You won't regret this, Sam. Thursday night still work for you?"

"Sure, but you'll have to convince her to do it. Good luck with that."

"I don't need luck." Her indignant tone filled his truck. "Watch your phone and I'll message you the details by midday Thursday. You won't regret this."

"Hope not. Gotta go." He ended the call and turned onto the highway out of town. Cindy was more like a younger sister than a cousin. He'd lived with Cindy's family on the ranch for a few years during elementary school. Dad's injuries from a workplace accident at a mill had forced their temporary relocation to the ranch.

Mom had worked long hours at two jobs in Colorado to pay their bills. Aunt Lori had homeschooled him, Uncle Joe had taught him how to be a cowboy like him and his older cousins. Sam was a step closer to leaving Gilead and starting over on the Colorado ranch he called home. He no longer had family ties in Gilead. Last year, Dad and Mom had moved to a town closer to Wichita, where Dad's family lived.

He had his doubts that Cindy could twist the Aussie girl's arm and convince her to go on a blind date with him. If she was attractive and had a cool accent, she'd have guys at the college falling over themselves to date her. He'd pray for wisdom if Cindy managed to pull off her crazy plan and land him a blind date for Thursday night.

CHAPTER 2

The following afternoon, Bek sat in her comfortable desk chair in her dorm, notebook computer open, and her Old Testament history assignment displayed on the screen. It was due later today. She'd proofread the text and checked the bibliography was complete before submitting it online. Most of the typos she'd corrected were silly mistakes from when she'd slipped back into the habit of writing Australian English.

She stretched her arms, straightened her spine, and rolled her shoulders. This was the last semester she'd be studying and living on campus. She'd return to Australia in early June and search for a new job. A career-building job that was more challenging than the tour guide work she'd left behind when she'd moved to Kansas. Maybe her big brother, Zach, was right, and she should consider studying to obtain high school English and History teaching qualifications.

Her phone pinged with a new notification. She opened the Messenger app and skimmed the long message from Mum.

It was early morning in Australia so she'd reply later. Bek missed her family back home, and she was glad Mum had finally come to terms with her decision to study in Kansas.

Mum knew why she'd chosen to leave Australia, although she suspected Mum still blamed her older sister, Kelly, for the distressing situation that had unfolded. Kelly was the wild child who ran with the wrong crowd, and she'd introduced Bek to the guy who'd tried, and failed, to ruin Bek's life.

Bek couldn't hold Kelly responsible for his actions. She'd chosen to date Jarrod, knowing his interest in attending church might not be genuine, knowing he could be lying when he'd said he shared her faith. That had been her oldest sister, Mel's, assessment of the situation. She should have taken Mel's concerns more seriously. He was an actor, after all, and he'd fooled her for too many months.

She'd repented and accepted the consequences from her unwise and misguided choices. Six months away from Sydney had given her clarity to discern what had gone wrong, and how she could protect herself from being conned again. Each day she prayed she'd walk closer with Jesus and seek His will for her life.

Her phone pinged again. A photo of Billie wearing winter clothes at the beach filled her phone screen. She read the accompanying note. Pensacola in Florida, on the Gulf coast. Billie and her husband, Zach, planned to drive south along the Florida coast to warmer weather.

Last month, Bek had enjoyed her Christmas break from college with her parents and siblings in Hawaii. Zach had described their Hawaiian Christmas vacation as Bek traveling halfway home and extending the olive branch that had pacified Mum. Zach and Billie had traveled with Bek back to the mainland. They'd spent the New Year in Nashville and hired a SUV to tour the chilly Midwest until Bek's second semester classes started.

Zach understood why she'd wanted to spend a year at Bible college. He'd seriously considered going to Bible college himself prior to marrying Billie and had suffered through Mum's objections to him discarding his merchant banking career. Zach's support meant the world to Bek.

Her brother and Billie had visited several Bible colleges during their travels, including her college in Gilead. They'd soon visit a Bible college in Trinity Lakes, Washington, in the small town where their friend, Joel, was temporarily living and working.

A knock sounded on her door. "Who's there?" Bek called out.

"Cindy."

Bek opened her door and greeted her friend.

"How's your tooth today?" Cindy asked, her voice brimming with concern.

"So much better." She'd appreciated Cindy's help yesterday after she'd returned from the dental appointment.

"I'm glad." Cindy flicked her blonde ponytail back over her shoulder. "Have you finished the assignment?"

"Almost. Only proofreading to do."

"Great." Cindy smiled and made herself at home in Bek's armchair recliner. "I've just submitted mine, and that means we have time to talk."

"I always have time to talk with you. At least I can actually move my mouth and talk without pain today."

Cindy chuckled. "That's helpful, lol."

"It sure is." Bek had tried to put the perplexing encounter with the cowboy out of her mind. He'd seen her at her worst, with a partially swollen jaw and an inability to talk.

She swung around in her desk chair and pointed to her fridge. "I restocked your iced tea this morning."

"Thanks. I wish I could fit a fridge in my room."

"You can borrow mine anytime." Bek was a fussy eater. Her room was designed for two students to share, but it only included one bed and desk. When she'd moved in, Mum had helped her set up a recliner, fridge with freezer, and a small kitchen cupboard that doubled as a counter in the spare space.

Bek took advantage of the communal cooking facilities in the dorm kitchen, and Cindy often shared meals with Bek. Her American friends in the dorm primarily used the microwave and cafeteria for their meals and were amused by Bek's Aussie quirks.

Cindy popped the lid on an iced tea and grabbed a tumbler from Bek's cupboard. "Would you like a glass?"

She shook her head. "I'm good, thanks." She adored hot tea, but she could take or leave lemon-flavored cold tea. "What time will we leave for the ranch on Friday?"

"After lunch. I want to get there before dark."

"Sounds good." She'd heard all about Cindy's family home on a south-eastern Colorado ranch and looked forward to visiting over the upcoming three-day holiday weekend.

Bek had declined Cindy's invitation last year to join her family for Thanksgiving at the ranch. She'd fallen behind on her studies and had been struggling with anxiety and homesickness. She hadn't wanted to intrude on Cindy's family celebrations. A therapist had helped Bek deal with the emotional baggage she'd lugged across the Pacific Ocean and let go of past hurts. The forgiveness part of her healing journey was a work in progress.

Cindy reclined in the lounge chair, hoisting up the footrest. "I've exciting news for you!"

"Really?" Cindy was a big ideas person who wanted to save the world and fix every problem. If only that was possible.

"I've found the perfect guy to take you on a blind date."

"Huh." She stared at Cindy, her jaw falling slack. "I know we talked about that last week, but I didn't think you were serious. It's a crazy idea."

"I'm deadly serious, and I can vouch for this guy. He doesn't have a shady background or gold-digging intentions like that Aussie guy who took you for a ride."

Becky shook her head. "How can you know for sure? I'm not looking to get married."

"Funnily enough, that's what he said. He's not looking for a wife, and you're not looking for a husband. You can be friends and go on a date with no pressure or expectations."

There had to be a catch. There was always a catch when something sounded too good to be true. "How well do you know him? It's easy for some people to put on their best behavior in the same way they'd put on a jacket. They hide all the yucky stuff underneath."

Cindy laughed. "You're too funny. The only thing he's hiding under his jacket is a six-pack. I've known him forever because we grew up together. Sam's my cousin."

"Oh, he's family." That did put a different spin on things. Cindy was putting herself out there and risking family disharmony to set up this blind date. Was there something wrong with him?

Cindy nodded. "He's a few years older than us, and my favorite cousin. His family lived with us on the ranch for a few years when we were kids. My dad taught him how to work the ranch with my brothers."

Bek lifted her brows. "He's a cowboy, yet he can't get a date. Really?"

"He's not technically working as a cowboy."

"What does he do?" An unemployed cowboy didn't sound like a good prospect.

"Sam's a farm mechanic and lives in Gilead. He's a hard worker, and an all-around good guy."

"Which brings me back to my original question. If he's such a good catch, why's he single?"

"That's not my story to tell. He's been burned like you but in a different way, and he's reluctant to date."

Everyone had a story. Bek was jaded by the whole dating merry-go-round, and she didn't want a romantic entanglement of any kind. Her trip abroad was supposed to be a relationship-free zone where she could learn from past mistakes and reset for her return home.

"Cindy, honestly, I don't think I'm your girl. Your cousin would be better off meeting an American girl and exploring if there's potential for a future together. I've nothing to offer —"

"That's not true. I've told him a little bit about you, and he's interested."

"What do you mean by interested? He wants to go along with your crazy blind date idea."

"He does. Meet Sam at Heavenly Brew on Thursday night. Low key, no pressure. I can give you a ride there and back, since you don't have wheels."

"I'd get wheels if you all drove on the correct side of the road." She'd driven on country roads with Zach and Billie last week but had found it stressful. A blind date was more stressful than navigating Nashville rush hour traffic.

"Ha ha." Cindy grinned. "I can set up a coffee date for seven, or seven-thirty. What's your preference?"

She sighed. "You're not going to take no for an answer, are you?" Heavenly Brew was a drawcard. Her favorite coffee shop, and essential detour for good coffee during her morning walk.

"It'll do you good to get back in the dating saddle."

Cindy had a point. Eventually she'd need to break her self-imposed dating exile. An American guy she'd leave behind in a few months wasn't the worst idea. "Okay. One date. That's all I'm prepared to do."

"Sure thing." Cindy stood. "I'll make the arrangements. A casual coffee date. Nothing special."

"If you say so." Bek would meet the mysterious Sam on Thursday. They could talk for an hour while she drank hot chocolate. Cindy would get off her case and drop the whole dating thing. A second date, or a romance of any description, was not going to happen.

～

ON THURSDAY EVENING, Sam carried empty pizza boxes and plates into his kitchen. Pete had stopped by with pizza for dinner, and they'd watched a replay of the Chief's football win. Monday was pizza night during the season, and a few of Sam's guy friends would visit after work for pizza and the game. Who'd have thought a big screen TV would improve his social life?

Pete had started stopping by on Thursdays after work while his fiancée, Emma, spent time with her sisters and friends. Sam suspected Pete wanted a break from his older brother and sister-in-law, Matt and Miley, who were working for the family business and staying with his folks until their new home was built. A three-month engagement followed by a Thanksgiving wedding hadn't given Matt and Miley enough time to find their first home. Pete and Emma had announced their engagement over a year ago and started planning their wedding in the dying months of Sam's long-distance relationship with Miley.

Pete entered the kitchen and placed more dishes by the sink. "Can I help?"

"Yeah, ice cream's in the freezer."

"Chocolate, I hope." Pete grinned. "Em has put us on a no-dessert diet, and it's killing me."

Sam chuckled. "Have you done the tux fitting?"

"Not yet. It's on February's list."

"Why the diet?" He passed Pete two bowls.

Pete scooped generous servings of chocolate ice cream at the kitchen island. "Em suggested it for a team-building exercise in our marriage preparation class. How could I say no?"

"Will she cheat by eating dessert, too?" He'd attempt a long run instead of his usual walk tomorrow, to burn the excess calories from Pete's super-sized serving. Assuming his knee would cope with the exertion.

"I doubt it." Pete paused, spoon in hand. "Em did her first fitting with the dressmaker before Christmas."

"Okay." He pulled out a stool to join Pete at the island. Miley used to fuss about her weight. She'd complained last year when he'd sent a Valentine's chocolate box to her Illinois college, unaware she was on a new sugar-free diet. He'd been hurt by her reaction to his gift. Now, he was glad he'd dodged a bullet. Miley was Matt's problem.

"Speaking of fittings and tuxes, I need your final answer to the question." Pete's phone beeped and he checked the screen. "Hold that thought. Gotta call a client." He stood and left the kitchen.

Sam continued eating ice cream. Pete and Matt were realtors in their father's firm, and clients calling during dinner was normal.

Pete was stuck in the middle. When Pete had asked Sam to be a groomsman a year earlier, neither of them had imagined that Sam and Miley would split, much less that Miley would marry Matt prior to Pete and Emma's wedding.

Sam wanted to bail on the groomsman duties, and Pete had held out hope that Sam would change his mind. How could Sam participate in the wedding knowing Miley was Pete's sister-in-law?

Years ago, Sam and Matt had been friends. They'd attended the same church and played together on the high school football team. Matt was a year older, the star quarterback who never lacked female attention.

Matt had changed colleges and switched majors after he was injured and lost his football scholarship. Sam had thought it was good that Matt had chosen to attend the same Illinois college as Miley. Good, right up until Matt had swooped in and charmed Miley into falling for him.

During Miley's final year at college, Sam had been a fool not to see the signs that their relationship was on the rocks. Miley had broken up with Sam after spring break last year and announced in June that she was in a relationship with Matt.

Pete returned to the kitchen. "Sorry about that. I need an answer to the question."

The question that had been a problem between them since June. "I want to bail."

"I can't change your mind?"

He shook his head. "It's too awkward for everyone."

Pete frowned. "You'll still come to the wedding."

"Of course. I wouldn't miss yours and Emma's special day." He'd blend into the crowd, stay away from cameras, and try to avoid an awkward encounter with Miley. She was immature and didn't think before she opened her mouth. Cindy had described Miley as having no filter. Insensitive was Mom's description.

Pete sat opposite, his gaze serious. "I don't want Miley to drive you away."

"She won't." He'd survive being in close proximity with Miley. Somehow. If he could avoid her at church, he could avoid her at a wedding. Distance was a good idea.

Pete cleaned up his ice cream bowl. "Have you lined up a plus-one, now you're not in the bridal party?"

"Do I need a plus-one?"

"Em insists you do, to send a clear message to Miley that you've moved on. I'm with Em on this one."

He shook his head. "Miley marrying Matt was moving on. Why would Miley care about who I take to the wedding?"

"Miley shouldn't care, but Em said she's asking questions about you."

He nodded. Sam didn't want to know what Miley was doing. Miley was history. Last summer, he'd spent hours talking and praying with his pastor about the situation. He'd prayed Miley and Matt would be happy together. When Sam moved to the ranch, he could leave Gilead and the Miley mess behind, and start over.

Sam glanced at the time displayed on the oven. Five minutes to seven. He had plenty of time to change and make his way to Heavenly Brew for his blind date with the mysterious Becky.

"Pete, there's something I didn't tell you about this thing I'm doing tonight."

"What's happening?"

"Cindy talked me into going on a blind date."

Pete's eyes widened. "That's great news. She could be your plus-one. Problem solved."

He shrugged off Pete's enthusiasm. "I'll find out soon." The date could be a massive disaster. Why had he allowed Cindy to talk him into it? A blind date was a bad idea. He'd always been a bundle of nerves before a first date, let alone a blind first date.

"Don't scare her away." Pete grinned. "If Cindy has chosen her, she must have potential."

"We'll see." He had low expectations.

"I'll leave you to get ready. Have fun."

"I'll try." He farewelled Pete, and the reality of the wedding situation sank in. Pete and Emma were worried about Miley ruining their wedding. The former cheerleader had a history of attention-seeking grandstanding. Miley upstaging Emma on her wedding day would be entirely in character and would create unnecessary drama within Pete's family.

Cindy was right. This Becky girl might be the answer to all their prayers. He'd try to make a good first impression and hope he could talk her into friend-dating until after Easter.

He changed into dating-appropriate clothing and combed his hair. He was overdue for a haircut. If he was outdoors, his cowboy hat would hide the short curls that wouldn't sit in place without fussing with products. And fussing with hair products wasn't his thing. Keeping his hair shorter was a better plan.

He'd hate working in an office like Pete and having to style his hair to meet client expectations. City living, and all the fancy things that went with that lifestyle, was not for him.

He grabbed the keys for his truck, headed across town, and found a parking space on the street close to Heavenly Brew.

There was no way he could fit in dessert after that giant bowl of ice cream.

He greeted Noah, a ranch hand who'd walked past his truck. Sam spent his workdays repairing and servicing tractors and other machinery at farms and ranches out of town. He'd gotten to know the local farmers and their hands from his regular visits for routine maintenance.

It was now or never. Sam hopped out of his truck, making sure he had his wallet and phone. After locking the truck, he ambled along the sidewalk toward the café, cowboy hat firmly in place on his head. He mostly worked on farms with crops rather than livestock, so he wore the standard business logo baseball cap at work.

The cowbell clanged and Sam stepped inside the coffee shop, took off his hat, and scanned the familiar interior of Heavenly Brew. Couples and groups filled most tables in the dining room, and he wondered if he'd been stood up. It wouldn't be the first time and could be a blessing in disguise.

He glanced at his phone. He was right on time. Should he wait, or call it and take off? What was the blind date etiquette for no shows?

His phone pinged. A message from Cindy. His date would be arriving soon.

He caught the eye of a server behind the counter, the only server working tonight. They chatted for a few minutes, and Sam claimed a newly vacated table tucked away near the back corner while still maintaining a clear view of the front entrance.

He pulled out a chair and took a seat, his eyes fixed on the door. His hands were clammy, and he could feel his face was flushed despite the cool temperature he'd left outdoors.

Laughter and chatter bounced around the room off the hardwood surfaces. The aroma of coffee wafted in the air. His fingers tapped in rhythm with the soft background music. He was distracted and ready to bolt.

The cowbell jingled and a brunette hesitantly entered the coffee shop on her own. Maybe he wasn't the only one feeling jittery.

Her gaze scanned the room and locked on his, her eyes widening.

It couldn't be.

Pretty girl. The girl from the elevator.

She held his gaze and walked toward him, her smile bright. Maybe this date had potential after all.

CHAPTER 3

$\mathcal{B}$ek's breath hitched, her gaze drawn like a magnet to the handsome face across the room. The cowboy. Cindy's cousin was the cowboy from the elevator. And her blind date. Her smile required no effort as she made her way to his table toward the back of Heavenly Brew.

She could relax. He wasn't a creeper or anything awful like her overactive imagination had ruminated on since agreeing to the date. He'd chosen her favorite table. She often studied here, helped by a cup or two of Letty's divine coffee. There was a coffee maker and French press in the dorm, but it was easier to visit Letty and her crew who made coffee the way she liked it.

Sam held her gaze, his welcoming smile putting her at ease. Cindy would be thrilled if their blind date was a success.

He stood and extended his hand. "Hi, Becky."

"Hi, Sam." She shook his strong hand. "Sorry I'm late."

"Only a few minutes. All good." He pulled out a chair opposite where he'd been sitting.

"Thank you."

"You're welcome."

His smooth voice was a soothing balm on her strained nerves.

She spotted his cowboy hat perched on a spare chair at the end of their table. She'd seen cowboys wearing hats indoors, but she didn't know the etiquette. Sam didn't need the hat. She liked how his fair curls bounced in different directions.

She liked Sam, and she was open to the possibility of friendship. Cindy hadn't given her enough time to research blind date etiquette. Which topics of conversation were appropriate when romance and a second date weren't an option?

"How's your tooth?" he asked.

"Much better." She smiled, appreciating his thoughtful question. He remembered her from the elevator. "I can talk normally."

"I love your accent."

"Thanks." His compliment heightened the warmth in her cheeks. His accent was lovely, too. Compliment-filled banter and flirting, her usual first date experience with a guy trying to impress her, didn't seem to be Sam's style. He was refreshing and intriguing.

He tipped his head to the side. "We should order."

"Yes. I know what I want."

"Really?"

She nodded. "Hot chocolate."

"How about dessert or cake?"

She shook her head. "I had chocolate mousse at the dorm cafeteria."

"Nice." He sat back in his seat. "I've heard you're not a fan of the cafeteria."

"Yeah." How much information had Cindy shared with Sam? "It depends on the menu. I can cook in the dorm kitchen."

"You like cooking."

"I don't mind it. I prefer eating food I like, which usually means cooking it myself."

"Okay then, I'll go order."

"No." She'd pay for her own drink. No strings. No commitment.

His eyebrows lifted. "You've changed your mind about hot chocolate."

"No. I'll get my order. Our order. What would you like? Are you hungry?" She pressed her lips together, halting the flow of disjointed sentences. His engaging smile messed with her ability to think.

He laughed. "I'm good. A friend super-sized my ice cream serving."

"Oh, wow." She chuckled. "I like ice cream, but not that much."

"Yeah. How about we order together?"

"Sure." The awkward conversation would pass. Was Sam a talker? Would she be doing the heavy lifting in their conversation? Too many questions with no answers.

They headed to the counter, and Bek placed her order with a teen she didn't recognize. She stood to the side and Sam chose hot black tea. She hadn't picked him for a tea drinker.

They returned to their table and she placed her phone beside the napkin holder, screen down. She was too aware of Sam for her own good. A good thing it wasn't a real date. She'd pepper him with questions, wanting to get to know him.

The teen called their names, and Sam collected their beverages.

She stirred pink and white marshmallows into her hot chocolate. Between chocolate mousse and hot chocolate, she'd need to add an extra loop tomorrow morning to her walk around campus. Classes started at ten, which should give her time to stop by Heavenly Brew for coffee during her walk, rather than ordering takeout.

"That looks good," he said.

"It always is, but I don't indulge often."

"Fair enough." He sipped black tea, with no added sweetener.

"How's your tea?"

"Good."

"Do you drink coffee?"

He nodded. "Not this late."

"Same. I was surprised you chose hot tea. I add milk to hot tea."

He smiled. "Mom drinks tea this way. It's a family thing."

"I can relate." She sipped her hot chocolate. Mum would like Sam and his tea preferences. "I don't add milk to green tea."

He held his cup in the air. "I don't know about flavored tea. This works for me."

"Okay." What else could they talk about, other than tea and the weather?"

He leaned back in his chair, smile intact. "So, Becky, tell me about yourself."

She gulped a mouthful of hot chocolate. "What would you like to know?" It couldn't hurt to enjoy her one and only date with a cowboy. The tingles were there, and she could stare into his eyes all evening.

"Start with how you landed in Gilead. Why Kansas?"

She relaxed her grip on her hot chocolate mug. "It all started in Germany, during my European trip with Mum after I graduated high school."

"Sounds interesting."

She hoped so. "We were in Bavaria, and Mum wanted to see the famous castles. We love history and visiting castles is fun. Have you been to Europe?"

He shook his head. "One day. Maybe."

"The day trip tour included a stop in a small town that put on a passion play every ten years."

His eyes widened. "Oberammergau? My buddy, Pete, has visited there."

"Who's Pete?"

"The ice cream guy."

"You mean the generous ice cream server."

"That's him. His family vacationed there to watch the passion play."

"Wow, that would be amazing. We visited in December and I did see the theater. Our tour guide shared the town history, and I was fascinated by the idea of a passion play."

"And that's why you chose Gilead."

She nodded. "It was a sign. I'd been praying about where to study. A Bible college that held an annual passion play came in at the top of my list."

"Are you participating in the play? The auditions were this week."

"I've volunteered to help behind the scenes." The last thing she wanted was her face and name getting online attention.

"Stage crew, or something else?"

She wrinkled her brows. "I'm not sure. I lined up my volunteering last year to gain credit points. My understanding is the play is a big commitment with a lot of hours."

He nodded. "It can be intense."

"Do you volunteer?"

"I sure do. This will be my seventh year as part of the stage crew, helping with set moving. We could be working together."

She grinned. "It would be fun to know someone else at the play. Cindy and my other dorm friends are doing different projects for their extra credits."

"Cindy volunteered two years ago. She had a small on-stage role in the crowd scenes."

"She'd mentioned the play was fun and exhausting. I love the theater, and I'm prepared to put in the work."

"Have you done any acting?"

"No. Never. I'm not interested in acting." Or actors. Once burned, never again. "How about you? Have you been in front of the camera?" He had the looks to pull it off.

He chuckled. "I hate public speaking. All those people watching? Not for me."

"That's fair. Last year I picked up a tour guiding job. It was fun, but it would have been horrible if I hated talking into a microphone."

"Was that a tourist job in Australia?"

"Yeah — in Sydney, which is where I'm from. It had its moments because I'm a history major with limited foreign language skills and most of our guests were from Europe or Asia. What do you do for work?" Cindy had mentioned he fixed machinery.

"I'm a farm mechanic."

"What does that involve?"

"Spending a lot of time driving to farms and ranches."

"Do you do cowboy work?"

He grinned. "I grew up doing ranch hand work. Not so much these days."

"So the hat isn't for show." She pointed to the beige cowboy hat. "You really are a cowboy?"

"I am. Don't you have cowboys in Australia?"

"We have Jackaroos and Jillaroos. Their hats are a bit different."

"Interesting. I've heard about your massive outback ranches."

"We call them cattle stations."

"Okay." He drank his tea. "Does that mean you have sheep stations, too?"

"Good guess. They're located a long way from where I live."

"You're in the city, right?"

She nodded. "A beach suburb."

"Nice."

"Can you fix cars as well as farm machinery?"

"Do you need help with a car?"

She shook her head. "I don't need wheels. Everything is walking distance."

"I do work on cars. My uncle, Cindy's dad, taught me a few things. I've always liked fixing stuff."

She sipped her hot chocolate. "Do you have family in Gilead?"

"Not anymore, except for Cindy. Last year Mom and Dad moved closer to Wichita." He paused, his gaze serious. "Do you miss Australia?"

"I do. I'll be home in a few months."

He nodded. "In May, I think Cindy said."

"Early June is the plan." She'd be packing up her life in Gilead in less than five months.

"What are your plans for when you return home?"

"I'm not sure." She'd think about it when she returned to Sydney. No point worrying now. Mum and Dad would provide accommodation for as long as she needed, and it wasn't like her childhood home was small.

"Sam, I'm curious." The question trapped in her throat needed to be asked. "Why are we here tonight?"

He drank his tea, taking his time to answer. "What's your expectation? Why are you here?"

"Cindy's a good friend and your cousin. I didn't want to disappoint her." There. She'd said it. A favor for Cindy was her reason. What was his?

His lips twitched into a smile that could be hiding a snicker. "I appreciate your honesty."

"No worries. Why did you agree to this blind date?"

His eyes widened a fraction. "It's complicated. One reason was to get Cindy off my case."

She raised her mug. "We can agree on that."

"That's a start."

A start for what? His face was open and friendly. Cindy had said he wasn't looking for a romantic relationship. Her curiosity was in overdrive. What was his story?

She held his gaze. "Also, I've never been on a blind date and didn't know what to expect."

"Me either. I'm not very good at first dates, let alone blind dates."

"What do you mean?"

"How many first dates have you been on that didn't lead to a second date?"

"Are we counting horrible first dates I never wanted to repeat?"

"No. Only dates where you were interested, and the other person ghosted you."

"Let me think." She'd mostly dated guys from church social circles, and they'd mutually agreed that being friends was the best option. "One, maybe two."

"I've been on three disastrous first dates in the last six months."

"Ouch. That's not fun. What went wrong?"

He shrugged. "I was too quiet, maybe. I was nervous."

"You're not being quiet tonight."

"Good to know. I have a question."

"Sure." Why the serious tone?

"Are you interested in being friends who hang out together?"

"I'm not sure what you're asking. If you're catching up with Cindy, I'm happy to tag along."

"I need a plus-one for a wedding I have to go to on Easter Saturday."

"Cindy could do that."

He shook his head. "Not in this particular situation."

"Why not?" The wedding seemed like a big deal. If it was too complicated, he could decline the invite.

"The wedding is my buddy, Pete. We've been friends since high school."

"Are you in the bridal party?" That was one way to avoid needing a plus-one.

"No. I declined Pete's offer."

"Why?" If they were such good friends, why wouldn't Sam want to stand up beside Pete at the wedding?

"Pete's brother married the girl I dated for years."

She widened her eyes. "Let me get this straight. Your ex is now Pete's sister-in-law."

He slowly nodded. "We split up during spring break."

"A few years ago, I'm guessing." That was manageable. Time heals. At least, that was the platitude everyone had spouted at her.

"Spring break last year. They married at Thanksgiving."

Yikes. "That's awkward." Who moved on that fast? She had whiplash from thinking about it.

"So everyone is telling me."

Everyone was right. Poor guy. "What's Cindy's grand plan?" She could guess, but she'd rather hear from Sam.

"Cindy thinks it could be helpful if people think you and me are dating."

Dating. That was a big leap from friends-who-hang-out. "Do you want us to date?"

He shook his head. "No, but it couldn't hurt if people kind of made that assumption."

A fake relationship. This was the stuff of romance novels, not real life. "Why does Cindy think I'd agree to this arrangement?"

"She said you might want to change churches, and hanging out with me could be helpful."

"Did Cindy say why?"

"She said that's your business."

She nodded. "Cindy has a point." A couple of the college guys who attended her church were misguided in their thinking. They were convinced Bek was in Gilead to find a husband and believed they were suitable candidates. In recent weeks, one of them had become more pushy in their intentions to prove their suitability, despite Bek declining every dating opportunity. Why couldn't some men understand and accept that no means no?

"Many of the passion play volunteers attend my church. It's only for a few months."

"I need to think about it." This wasn't what she'd expected to be pondering at the end of their date.

"Can you let me know your answer on Monday?"

"Why Monday?" Did he have other candidates? That could explain his run of bad first dates.

"We'll be at the ranch all weekend with time to figure out if this arrangement could work."

Sam would be at the ranch?

Cindy had left out that important piece of information when she'd invited Bek. They could have avoided the whole date thing tonight. Although then she'd have missed out on a delicious hot chocolate and Sam's company.

He was a nice guy, and he'd been honest. It would be helpful to not have to deal with unwanted male attention at church and in her classes. She needed to pray about their situation. Their weekend at the ranch would be interesting.

THE NEXT MORNING, Sam carried a small box of vegetables to his truck. He'd started early at Bed of Greens Truck Farm, knowing he had a full morning of work to complete before driving to the ranch this afternoon.

He'd have lunch at home, after cleaning up and finalizing his timesheet and paperwork for his boss. Invoicing would be his job if he started his own farm mechanic business. There were pros and cons. It was easier to work for someone else, but once he moved to Colorado, he'd need more flexibility in his schedule to do ranch work and farm mechanic work. Flexibility would be easier if he was his own boss.

If Sam was quick, he might have time to get everything done and follow Cindy and Becky to Colorado. Cindy was a stickler for time and wouldn't delay her journey unless it was an emergency.

Connor waved and joined Sam at the truck.

"Thought you'd left earlier," Connor said.

"That was the plan."

"What happened?"

"Radiator hose in the old green tractor sprung a leak." He'd finished the scheduled maintenance tasks early and waited around for the tractor engine to cool. Thankfully, he'd found a replacement hose in his spare parts supplies.

"Not good." Connor checked out the box contents and chuckled. "Vegetables. Why do you need green stuff?"

He grinned. "My aunt. She asked me to pick up a few things."

"Doesn't she live on a ranch?"

"Yup. I'm following instructions." Who knew why she needed beets and squash? Uncle Joe had asked him to help the ranch hands tomorrow while his cousins were out of town for the weekend.

"Maybe she's putting you on a vegan diet."

"Not gonna happen. I know where to find steaks in the freezer."

Connor shook his head. "Good luck."

"Should be wishing you good luck. I heard your audition went well."

"I'll find out next week."

"You'll pick up a role." Most people who auditioned for the passion play landed a part.

"Hope so." Connor took a step back. "See you round."

"Don't eat too many greens for lunch."

"No way." Connor laughed and strode toward the shed.

Sam opened his truck rear door. He wedged the vegetable box on the floor behind the front passenger seat. The Groenings, who owned Bed of Greens, were good people, and they wanted Connor to participate in the passion play. It was on Sam's list to send his employer the rehearsal schedule and make the necessary adjustments to his work hours to accommodate the play.

Mrs. Alleghany had made her presence known in Heavenly Brew this morning. She'd talked non-stop about the auditions to whoever would listen. According to Mrs. Alleghany, Connor had competition for the Judas role. Sam had heard that tidbit of interesting information while waiting for Letty to make his coffee. If Sam was an actor, Judas would be the last role he'd want to perform in the play.

Sam fired up his truck, hit the road, and checked the time. He'd arrive home around the same time as Cindy and Becky would be leaving town. No chance of catching them or meeting at their favorite diner along the way. The rate he was going, with all the delays, he'd be stopping at the diner for an early fried chicken dinner instead of an afternoon snack. Cindy liked the diner's salad selection. Too much green for him.

He turned up the radio volume, switching between the contemporary Christian and country music stations. He'd need to check the weather before leaving Gilead. Today was mild for January, but snow showers were a possibility at this time of year.

His blind date last night with Becky had turned out better than he'd anticipated. His nerves had settled after he'd recognized her from the elevator, and he talked more when he wasn't stressed. Becky was cute, and she seemed like a nice girl. Very different to Miley. And she hadn't given him an outright no to his plus-one wedding guest proposal. He'd need to thank Cindy for arranging the date.

Interestingly, he hadn't heard from Cindy today. A good sign that he hadn't scared Becky off, and that Becky was taking his wedding dilemma seriously. Cindy, and most of his family, didn't have good things to say about Miley. When Miley had gone public with her relationship with Matt, Sam's family hadn't held back on sharing their thoughts.

One day, Gilead and the Miley situation would be a distant memory in his rearview mirror. Uncle Joe had allocated time this weekend to go over the ranch finances and share his plans for future investments in stock and ranch infrastructure. Sam hoped that conversation included an opportunity to discuss a location for Sam's dream home. The homestead was large and, like his cousins, he wanted to build his own place. Then Dad might visit the ranch more often than a short annual Christmas trip, and Mom would be happier.

He'd talk to Cindy about keeping his friendship with Becky under wraps. The last thing he wanted was their moms talking about Becky, and his mom hatching wedding and grandbaby plans. It was a temporary arrangement. Nothing more. It helped that Becky was a beautiful woman with a to-die-for accent. Their mutual attraction would make a potential romantic relationship more believable. If Mrs. Alleghany had been at Heavenly Brew last night, the whole town would have him married off to Becky by dinnertime.

His first step was to convince Becky to be his plus-one for the wedding. Then he could take the second step and RSVP with Becky as his plus-one. Pete anticipated Emma's family would send out the wedding invitations next week. Sam's third step, and the most important step. Don't fall in love with Becky. That could end up being the hardest step to follow.

CHAPTER 4

*B*ecky tossed her overnight bag into the back of Cindy's SUV. There were advantages to having the same clothing and shoe size as Cindy. She'd borrow Cindy's ranch apparel and, for the first time in years, indulge in her childhood love for horse riding. It was a holiday weekend, and they'd spend three nights at the ranch, returning to Gilead on Monday after lunch.

Cindy stowed a Sew Easy cloth bag. "I almost forgot the fabric Mom ordered."

"Then you'd be in trouble." A teasing tone infused her voice. She liked Cindy's mom and looked forward to visiting with her.

"Zoey sent me a reminder this morning."

"That was helpful." The Gilead retailers looked after their customers, an appealing aspect of small-town life that she appreciated.

"The crafty gene skipped my generation."

She snickered. "That's why we're friends. My mum knits. I can sew, but it's not my jam."

"I can relate. Zoey's assisting with wardrobe at the play."

"Good for her. I can watch the performances and move props.

More fun than sewing backstage." She'd received an email this morning, confirming her volunteer schedule for stage crew.

"That's fair. I was done with sewing after a machine needle zoomed through the tip of my fingernail."

"I don't want to know how you managed that feat." She shoved her hands further into the pockets of her padded jacket, thankful her fingertips were safe from Cindy and a rogue sewing machine.

Cindy laughed. "Fortunately that fingernail was long. Mom fixed it." Her phone beeped and she checked the screen. "Sam's been delayed at work."

"He's coming with us?"

"No, but we often drive together and stop at our favorite diner on the way."

"We could wait for him." Would she be paired with Sam at the play? Too many warm tingles accompanied that thought. She hadn't made a decision on the plus-one wedding invitation. The old Bek in Sydney would have dived straight in and agreed to attend without considering the consequences. The new Becky in Gilead wanted to consider all the implications first. Seek wise counsel first. Pray first.

"He's running way behind." Cindy frowned. "Let's go now. I hate driving west at sunset."

"Sure." She walked around to the passenger door. Cindy was punctual to a fault, and last night she'd chastised Becky for keeping Sam waiting at Heavenly Brew. Who turned up early for first dates, let alone blind dates?

Minutes later, they were traveling on the road out of town. Never-ending miles of flat plains and cornfields surrounded the highway. Did Kansas have vivid yellow canola fields that bloomed during spring? Their detour to the diner, and a small serving of Greek salad with her afternoon coffee, was a pleasant distraction.

Cindy filled their travel time with her new country music

playlist. After visiting Nashville, Becky had shared her ignorance of all things country music. Cindy was on a mission to rectify that situation, and Becky was a captive audience during their road trip.

They crossed the state line into Colorado and gained an hour by moving to Mountain Time.

Her phone updated the time. "It's weird switching time zones in winter."

"Huh. Don't you have different time zones in Australia?"

"We do, but the eastern states are all in the zone during winter. Summer is different, with daylight savings."

"Daylight savings is confusing."

"It sure is." Her phone app with the different world time zones came in handy.

Cindy swung her SUV off the highway and they traveled further into ranch country. Paddocks and cattle with occasional horses made up the bulk of the scenery.

"Can we see the Rockies from the ranch?"

"Sorry, we're too far east. Colorado is a big state." Cindy flipped the blinker and slowed the vehicle. "Welcome to the ranch."

"It's lovely." They cruised along the drive toward a sprawling single-story house with a wide, welcoming verandah, and low-pitched roof. Wood featuring and hanging flower baskets added color and character.

Cindy drove around the back, where a greenhouse and sheds were located. "We'll unload here."

"Okay." Becky hopped out of the SUV, glad to stretch her legs, and drew in a deep breath. The air was cold and dry, but somehow different to Kansas. A faint aroma she associated with cattle lingered in the dusty breeze. The sun was closing in on the western horizon. A light cloud cover previewed pastel-toned displays of God's handiwork. She was blessed to have an opportunity to spend the weekend here.

"You made it." Cindy's mom walked over from the veranda and hugged her daughter, then embraced Becky in a warm hug. "Come on in. We'll have refreshments outdoors and watch the sunset. Dinner is beef stew."

"Sounds great." Becky helped carry their luggage inside and admired the open plan design. A large-screen TV was surrounded by sofas and recliners, and a twelve-seat dining table filled the living area closest to the kitchen. Family photos were on prominent display on the shelves, with men in cowboy gear a common theme. Becky spotted a photo of a younger Sam holding his cowboy hat.

Cindy's mom, Lori, made a beeline to the kitchen beyond the dining area. The modern space was enormous, with a generous-sized marble topped island and breakfast bar with wooden stools in the middle. A functional eight-burner cooktop, twin ovens, and large fridge were surrounded by cupboards, and there was plenty of space for food preparation. A slow cooker exuded a lovely rich beef aroma. Her stomach grumbled, and she couldn't wait to taste the stew.

A door off the kitchen opened into a large pantry with floor to ceiling shelving. Mum would love this kitchen. Becky loved the expensive espresso machine on the counter.

Lori placed three mugs on the counter beside the machine. "Girls, what would you like?"

"Decaf latte please," Cindy said.

"Same for me. Thank you." Despite their plans to cook late into the evening, decaf was a better option. She was limiting her caffeine intake and not having anything caffeinated after four in the afternoon.

"You're welcome. Cindy can give you the tour while I whip these up."

Becky followed Cindy along a long hall to a well-appointed guest room. French doors opened onto a verandah that wrapped around the homestead. Horses grazed in a nearby field. The wide-open spaces reminded her of Australian farms.

She returned to the kitchen with Cindy and carried a coffee mug to a door facing west. She was glad she'd worn her favorite sweater, a long cable-knit design Mum had hand knitted. She curled up in a cushioned chair on the veranda, pulling her sleeve cuffs over her hands, and cradling her latte.

"Have the boys already left?" Cindy asked.

Lori nodded and sipped her hot tea. "Their plans changed this morning, and they'll be back Monday morning."

Cindy smiled. "It'll be quiet without them."

"Sam called, and he's arriving after dinner. I'll put stew aside," Lori said.

Becky nodded, her attention drawn to the stunning sunset colors lighting up the wispy clouds. This place was peace and serenity wrapped up in a pretty package. She was a million miles away from her problems in Australia.

Cindy's three older brothers were out of town for a friend's wedding. Sam would fill in on the ranch and help his uncle.

"Girls, I have everything ready for you to cook tonight. A few days in the freezer, and your meals will travel well in the cooler bag back to Gilead."

Cindy smiled. "Thanks, Mom."

"I appreciate your hospitality, and your kitchen." They'd brought a supply of glass storage containers to fill her freezer multiple times. Nutritious frozen meals, shared with Cindy, would be a time saving blessing during the passion play season leading up to Easter.

"You're welcome." Lori stood. "Enjoy the sunset while I finish our dinner preparations."

Becky stretched in her seat, content to chat with Cindy about her childhood experiences on the ranch. One older brother was enough when Becky was growing up, and she couldn't imagine three of them bossing her around.

Cindy's dad, Joe, stopped by the veranda and updated them on his day. It was thankfully uneventful, other than fixing a broken water pump at the dam. A different world to her city life in Sydney. Water was a precious commodity on a working ranch.

Dinner was served. Becky sat beside Cindy at one end of the dining table, opposite Cindy's parents. The tasty beef stew, chock-full of fresh and wholesome ingredients, filled her stomach and satisfied her appetite.

She dabbed her mouth with her napkin. She loved the informality and the easy way Cindy related to her parents. In hindsight, she should have accepted Cindy's invitation to visit the ranch for Thanksgiving instead of moping around campus by herself. Those hard days were behind her, and she appreciated the warm welcome and exceptional hospitality.

Joe smiled. "Sam's working with the ranch hands from dawn. We'll be out all day, and back at sunset."

"A long day in the saddle." Cindy wrinkled her nose. "Glad it's him, not me."

"You're more capable than you think," he said.

"I like being able to walk without pain."

"There's that." He grinned. "Or toughen up and regain your strength."

"I'm doing okay."

"Sitting in front of a screen isn't doing you good. You're riding tomorrow?"

Cindy nodded. "A short ride. Becky hasn't been near a horse in years."

"We can fix that." Joe turned to Becky. "Do you know your way around a horse?"

"I know not to walk behind them."

He chuckled. "That's a start. Can you ride?"

"I could when I was a kid. We'll see if muscle memory is a real thing."

Lori held her spoon mid-air. "Where did you learn?"

"Family friends own a horse stud near Sydney."

Joe sipped his water. "You're lucky to have that opportunity."

She nodded. "It was fun." Her parents' old school friends had built a lavish country mansion and lived like royalty. Their horse stud wasn't homely and welcoming like Cindy's family ranch.

Cindy's father was the quintessential cowboy, and everything Becky had imagined in a career rancher. He kept them entertained with witty conversation about life on the ranch. Who knew the antics of cows could be interesting?

Becky glanced over at the living room, watching the time tick over on the tall antique grandfather clock. Sam was due anytime. Lori had put aside a serving of stew, and they'd have pie for dessert after Sam arrived. Becky could understand why Sam didn't want to miss out on dinner.

She helped Cindy clear the table, rinse the dishes, and load the dishwasher. She poked around the pantry with Lori, fascinated by the vast collection of glass jars full of preserved fruits and vegetables from last year's harvest. The large glass jars of tomatoes would be awesome in her pasta sauce.

Becky picked up a jar of marinated olives. "Your pantry is like a farmers market stall."

"I enjoy doing the preserving, but it is time consuming."

"But so worth it. On Sundays, after church, I'd visit a nearby farmer's market with my friends and meet Mum there. She'd bring her walking trolley bag, and we'd stock up on organics."

"Does your mother attend church?" Lori asked.

Becky gulped. "Sometimes. It's complicated." Mum was burned by bad experiences, years ago. When Mum was worked up about church issues, it wasn't fun being on the receiving end. Dad claimed he was too busy for church. His schedule as a surgeon was crazy and unpredictable.

"We'll head into town for Sunday service, followed by a late lunch here. We rest on Sundays, unless there's an emergency."

"Sounds like a plan." According to Cindy, the small church in town held lovely services. Becky looked forward to a new church experience, worshiping with Cindy's family and congregation.

Cindy poked her head into the pantry. "Let's get started on our meal prep before Sam arrives."

"Sure," Becky said.

Cindy and her mom had worked out a plan to cook a range of meals tonight and tomorrow that could be frozen. Cindy returned home at least once a month, often for family celebrations, and she could bring back a new supply of meals to top up Becky's freezer.

Her play schedule would make it harder to find time to cook in the dorm. Easy and nutritious soups, stews, and pasta dishes would be helpful. Becky picked the short straw and gained the fun job of slicing multiple pounds of onions. Her eyes watered, and she grabbed her sunglasses from her purse.

Lights flashed outside and Lori smiled. "That would be Sam."

The back door opened, and Sam strolled inside, luggage in tow, and his cowboy hat hiding his unruly curls.

"Hey." Becky stood and joined the chorus of welcomes.

Sam greeted everyone then pointed at Becky's face. "Sunglasses at night."

She grinned. "It beats onion tears."

"Why not use bagged chopped onion from the store?"

"Nope. I avoid precut. It's cheaper to chop the fruit and veggies myself, and it's easy enough."

He nodded. "I'll be back soon."

Lori turned on an oven and set the timer. "Joe and I have a few things to do. We'll be back shortly for dessert."

Cindy nodded. "No problem. I'll watch the apple pie."

Sam returned indoors and placed a cardboard box on the kitchen counter.

"What's in here?" Cindy looked inside. "Veggies."

"Your mom asked me to pick up a few things from Bed of Greens."

"How thoughtful. Thank you." Cindy turned to Becky. "Last summer was dry, and Mom cut back on what she grew."

She nodded. "Thanks, Sam. Would you like to join our big cook up?"

He raised his hands. "I'm not good in the kitchen."

Cindy chuckled. "What he's trying to say is he doesn't knowingly eat vegetables and probably couldn't even name everything in the box."

"Oh." She flipped her sunglasses on her head and narrowed her eyes. "You really don't eat veggies?"

"I eat fries." He filled a bowl with a generous serving of beef stew and pulled out a stool at the island.

"Who doesn't, lol. Fries don't count." She scraped a pile of sliced onion onto a plate and started chopping bell peppers.

"They should count." He ate a mouthful of stew. "There's vegetables in the stew. I can taste beef, which is what matters."

Becky shook her head. "You're missing out. Veggies are delicious and full of important nutrients."

He shrugged. "Mom isn't a great cook. Years of soggy and tasteless vegetables turned me off for life."

Cindy picked out beets from the box. "My aunt has worked long hours nursing for as long as I can remember. No time for cooking."

"That's true." Sam ate another mouthful of stew. "Mom often worked night shift. Box mac and cheese was an easy option."

Blech. Becky's stomach churned but she stayed quiet, holding her tongue in check. Who was she to judge? Money hadn't been a problem at home. Dad's lucrative career as a surgeon, combined with inherited money, had given Mum choices. Mum chose not to return to work after Zach was born.

Mum had considered homeschooling when Kelly was in trouble and running with the wrong crowd. Becky had factored in homeschooling as a good reason for obtaining teaching qualifications, even if she'd never work in a classroom.

Sam finished his stew, almost scraping the bowl clean. "That was good."

The oven timer beeped, and they took a break from food preparation for apple pie and ice cream. Cindy's parents and Sam retired for the night, and the girls continued cooking.

Cindy closed the door leading to the hall. "Now we can talk. Have you made a decision about the wedding?"

She added water to the sink, chose a few potatoes, and picked up the scrubbing brush. "I'm praying about it. I learned a painful lesson last year, and I don't want to hurt Sam."

"How is being Sam's plus-one going to hurt him?"

"He might think he's happy and doesn't want a real relationship, but what if he changes his mind?" What if she changed her mind? The tingles that led to trouble bubbled in the background whenever they were together.

"I guess you pray about it, and cross that bridge if it happens. Sam's telling the truth. He's not looking for love."

"What is he looking for?" The big question that bugged her. Was there an ulterior motive? Was she overthinking the situation?

"He needs to survive being near Miley at the wedding." Cindy chopped carrots at the island.

"Why's the wedding such a big deal?" Plenty of people went to weddings on their own.

"It's Miley." Cindy sighed. "Gilead is a small town. Too small, sometimes."

"What do you mean?" She plucked potatoes out of the sink.

"I briefly dated a guy from church who was good friends with Matt."

"Miley's husband?"

"Yup." Cindy moved the chopped carrots to a plate. "He went to the same college as Miley."

"Why's that important?"

Cindy's frown deepened. "It was a few years ago, when Sam

was still in a long-distance relationship with Miley. The guy I was dating told me Miley had hit on him. She'd wanted a casual fling. He said no, of course."

Miley might be a cheater. Charming. "How'd you know he's telling the truth?"

"He showed me the text messages. I had Miley's number in my phone, and the numbers plus her weird abbreviations matched."

"Wow." Becky had more in common with Sam than she'd realized. "Does Sam know about this?"

Cindy shook her head. "I couldn't tell him. At that time he was only seeing Miley when she returned to Gilead during college breaks. I figured Sam would work it out himself, break up with her, and move on."

"Is that what happened?" She hoped and prayed he'd moved on. Sam didn't seem like the type of guy who'd hold out hope for reconciling with his newly married ex-girlfriend.

Cindy shook her head. "Not exactly. It didn't take long for Miley to dump Sam and move on with Matt."

"Oh." Miley sounded like a piece of work. Sam had a lucky escape, from the sounds of it. "What does this mean for the Easter wedding?"

"Miley might try to mess with Sam's head. Matt will be busy with best man stuff, and Miley isn't in the bridal party. She's a man-eater and Sam will be a vulnerable target if he's on his own."

Becky found a large saucepan. "I can't see Sam having anything to do with Miley." He had integrity.

"You haven't met Miley. For years she had Sam all wrapped up in her."

"I'll think on it." Sam seemed sincere in his faith, and he was a regular church attender. He wasn't a fake, wasn't a player, wasn't a cheater. He wasn't like Jarrod.

Sam's close friend being Miley's brother-in-law made it more complicated. Miley being unfaithful with Sam would blow up the extended family.

Cindy's heart was in the right place. She wanted Sam protected from Miley's wandering ways. Could Becky maintain a healthy friendship with Sam that stayed in the friend zone? Could she help Sam and protect her own heart?

CHAPTER 5

*L*ate on Saturday afternoon, Sam rode with Uncle Joe along a perimeter fence. They'd check the fencing was intact and doing its job of keeping the cattle in.

He'd woken early and had oatmeal for breakfast with the ranch hands before heading out to start their day. Ranching had a different routine and pace of work to his farm mechanic job. Most days, he spent more time driving his truck from place to place than actually fixing stuff.

He'd enrolled in a new mechanic course, starting after Easter, to update his farm machinery technology skills. Computers ran the world and that included farm machinery. He'd rather be on a horse and appreciating the natural beauty of God's creation.

His day had run smoothly. After lunch, Uncle Joe had shown him the ranch accounts and provided an overview of their operations. The ranch was in a good financial situation. External assets were in place to provide a financial buffer during drought and other rough years.

He'd discovered Mom was in the process of selling off a portion of her share. She wanted a lump sum to top up her retirement fund. He was frustrated he'd learned this information from his uncle rather than Mom.

Sam could sell his house in Gilead, which only had a small mortgage owing. He could invest more funds in the ranch or do something else with the house sale proceeds. Big decisions. He'd need to seek independent financial advice.

He slowed the mare to a gentle walk and turned to his uncle. "I've been thinking over our conversation. Am I right in assuming I could let the inheritance roll along and stay in Gilead?"

"That's correct. Your grandfather set up his will to ensure you'd have the option to work on the ranch if that's what you wanted. The ranch can absorb the cost of your mother selling more of her share."

"What do you mean? Has she previously sold her shares?"

Uncle Joe steered his horse closer, facing him, his expression serious. "I thought you knew."

He shook his head, pulling down his hat rim to block the sun. "When?"

"A few times over the years."

"Since Dad's accident." The puzzle pieces were jolting into place like an earthquake shifting the ground. Dad had avoided visiting the ranch and avoided seeing Mom's family for a reason.

"Since she moved back to Kansas. Most years she's chipped away at her share, needing extra funds for stuff."

That stuff would have included the cost of raising him. At least Mom hadn't been burdened with college tuition. Money was tight when Sam was growing up, and getting a college education had never been on his radar. Academic pursuits weren't his thing.

Dad's physical injuries from the workplace accident may have healed, but the debilitating depression and anxiety remained. Maybe those health issues had always been there, and the work accident had exacerbated the situation.

The upshot was Dad hadn't returned to work full-time and had only worked the occasional odd job. Mom and the ranch had saved their family from financial ruin.

"Why didn't Mom tell me?"

His uncle stroked his beard, his gaze thoughtful. "Your parents are proud people. Especially your dad. He wouldn't be happy about our conversation."

He nodded. "So Mom's inheritance is smaller now."

"It doesn't matter. She can move back to the ranch. Anytime. Our door is always open."

"Thanks for telling me the truth." Mom's family were an open book and believed in straight talking. His relationship with Dad was complicated. Dad wouldn't discuss the ranch, or Sam's inheritance.

"You deserve the truth, son."

Sam groaned. "A whole lot of stuff makes sense now." He could read between the lines. Uncle Joe wasn't happy about Mom's financial decisions or his father's role in why Mom had gradually sold off her share in the ranch.

Dad had been a bigger burden on the family finances than Sam had realized. If Dad had recovered fully from his workplace injuries, and not wallowed in depression and relying on Mom to carry the financial burden, their retirement situation would be a different story.

Now their decision to downsize last year made sense. Their decision to move to a smaller home in a town near Wichita where Dad had grown up made sense. Dad's reluctance to visit Colorado made sense. The spike in tension in his parents' marriage also made sense.

His horse skittered. She could probably feel the stress in his body. Perceptive creature. A bolting horse wasn't what he needed.

"Easy girl." He stroked the mare's neck, calming her with soft words.

"I'd no idea things were that bad financially for my parents," Sam said.

Uncle Joe stared off into the distance. "I'm often not in agreement with your father. We've had our differences, and I've always tried to do right by you and my sister."

He'd long suspected Dad was jealous of Uncle Joe, and jealous of Sam's close relationship with Mom's Colorado family — an undeniable truth that had added unnecessary complications to their extended family relationships.

Sam continued stroking the mare's neck. "I've tried to stay out of it, and not land in the middle."

"Your mother will make good decisions. I've always made sure she's okay."

"I appreciate your support." Making lemonade from lemons was Mom's specialty, both literally and figuratively.

"You're like a son to me, Sam. Please know you aren't wedded to living here, now or in the future. You want to build a house and put down roots. I understand that, but the house could be a vacation home. You could stay in Gilead, or live somewhere else."

He blew out a long breath. *The world is your oyster.* Mom's favorite saying, despite her seafood allergy. She'd encouraged him to spread his wings and live the life God had planned.

Sam didn't want to stay in Gilead. His history with Miley had made everything awkward. He didn't want to move to the town where Dad's family lived. Too close to the city. Too far to commute and continue with farm mechanic work.

Uncle Joe kept his gaze on the fence line. "Becky seems like a nice girl."

"She is, and she's Cindy's friend." He'd spend the weekend reinforcing this fact.

"I heard you took her out on a date a few days ago."

"We spent an hour at Heavenly Brew. We're friends."

His uncle rode closer to the fence. "Something has tried to get through here."

"The fence is holding." The ground was freshly dug on the other side. He couldn't see animal tracks.

Uncle Joe pulled out his phone and took a few photos. "I'll get one of the boys to check in here on Monday."

"I can check it Monday morning. My cousins might want the day off."

"Good point. I'll send you the photos and map coordinates."

"That works." He could ask Becky if she'd like to go horseback riding. During lunch, Cindy had filled him in on their dinner conversation last night. Becky claimed to have horseback riding skills, and he was curious. The more time he spent with her, the more likely she was to agree to be his plus-one. That was his theory, and he was sticking to it.

"About Becky." His uncle looked him straight in the eye. "She seems smitten with ranch life."

"Smitten." Really? Who used that word to describe a ranch?

"Lori's description. If you aren't interested in her, she has ideas of marrying Becky off to one of the boys."

"Hang on. Who's talking about marriage?" He wasn't sure how he felt about the idea of one of his cousins dating Becky. She was cute, and they'd likely fight over her.

Uncle Joe chuckled. "You know what women are like. Becky has cooked up a storm with Cindy, filling the freezer with gourmet food."

He shook his head. "Cindy set us up on a blind date. Becky is thinking about being my plus-one for Pete and Emma's wedding."

"I hope she says yes."

"Why? How do you know about the wedding?"

"Your aunt talks. We aren't Miley fans, and Becky would be helpful in keeping her away. A good result."

"Becky's going home to Australia in a few months."

His uncle grinned. "Keep an open mind. Good women who love the Lord aren't a dime a dozen."

He nodded. He'd made a mistake in thinking Miley was a woman of strong faith. He wouldn't make that same mistake twice. Becky had him pinned in the friend zone, and that suited him.

"Becky could adapt to ranch life. Or you could explore Australia. The ranch isn't your only option."

Ranch life, and this land, had invisible strings pulling him closer. He could build a future here with support from Mom's family. Provide a place for Mom to stay when she visited. Build a house where Dad might stay for longer than a few nights over Christmas. He couldn't picture Becky being happy on a ranch. He prayed God would open the door to his destiny and lead him into a future within His will.

On Monday morning, Becky sat in a chair on the veranda and pulled on the cowboy boots she'd borrowed from Cindy. She'd meet Sam at the stables soon and join him for a morning ride. During breakfast, she'd declined a serving of grits. Who knew why Sam liked grits, but didn't like vegetables? She'd enjoyed Canadian bacon and eggs with sourdough toast. A family breakfast that reminded her of home. The whole weekend reminded her of home.

After breakfast, Cindy and her mom began planning an upcoming family birthday celebration. Cindy had aunts, uncles, and cousins all over Colorado and Kansas.

Cindy and Lori had encouraged Becky to make the most of an opportunity to go riding with Sam before returning to Gilead this afternoon. It almost felt like a setup. It probably was a tactic to push them together. She suspected Cindy had inherited her matchmaking streak from her mother.

Becky breathed in the crisp cattle country air and looked out at the paddocks. Birdsong wafted through the air. On Saturday afternoon, they'd finished cooking and storing meals. Lasagna, pasta sauces, stews, and soup were all stored in glass containers in the freezer.

Ranch life was different to what she'd imagined. There was always stuff happening, always people coming and going. Sam had spent Saturday working, and she'd seen him briefly at lunchtime. On Sunday morning, they'd traveled into town to attend a lovely service at a historic church. Becky appreciated the small town's history and heritage.

Sunday at the ranch was a day of rest. They'd played board games during the afternoon and watched movies. It was years since her family had done anything similar. By the time she was thirteen, her older siblings were out all weekend and doing their own thing.

She stood and stretched out her back muscles. Her lower back and legs had mild aches from her short ride with Cindy on Saturday afternoon.

The ground crunched underfoot as she made her way to the stables. Sam walked toward her, leading two horses.

He smiled. "Right on time."

"Of course. I'm looking forward to it."

She stroked the neck of a beautiful chestnut mare. Caro was a sweet and gentle girl, who Becky had fallen in love with on Saturday. Sam needed to check a perimeter boundary fence, which was a longer ride than Saturday.

"Meet Beauty." Sam's smile widened, highlighting his dimple. "She's one of my favorite horses."

"She's beautiful." Becky gave the tall mare some attention, and Beauty whinnied her appreciation.

"Do you need help getting into the saddle?" he asked.

She shook her head. "I'm good." She put her left foot in the stirrup, swung her right leg over the horse, and settled in the saddle. The western saddle was different to the smaller English-style saddle she'd ridden in Australia. She could wind rope around the saddle horn. One of the many differences she'd discovered during her online research after her ride with Cindy.

Sam handed her the reins and, in one fluid motion, he was in his saddle.

Smooth. The man knew his way around horses.

"We'll take it easy and walk to the fence line."

"Sure." Her legs appreciated warm up time in the saddle. Tomorrow she'd feel like a long soak in a bath. At home, she'd have enjoyed indulging in the spa bath at her parent's home.

His horse walked beside hers, and he turned toward her, cowboy hat and sunglasses hiding his gaze. "Where did you learn to ride?"

"At a horse stud."

"In Sydney."

"Nearby. Family friends lived in the Southern Highlands." She had great memories of riding up and down the rolling hills on their beautiful property.

"That sounds fun. Was it a large land holding?"

She nodded. "A gorgeous historic homestead. Prime real estate." Their old family friends were now a billionaire family. Smart investments over the years in green energy and other business ventures had paid off and elevated them into the uber-rich category. Mum had thought it hilarious that she had billionaire friends who lived like normal people. Although Mum's definition of normal was debatable.

"Do you visit often?" he asked.

"Not anymore. Which is sad."

"What happened?"

"My sister. Kelly. Something happened to her." Her parents had decided it was best to stay away. They now visited their friends in Queensland at their beachfront mansion.

"Was she injured horseback riding?"

"No. Nothing like that. A situation with a stable hand didn't end well." Becky had been away at a school camp and missed all the drama. Kelly had just turned sixteen and was caught using drugs with a nineteen-year-old guy.

"Oh. Was she okay?"

"Sort of. Mum was furious. Kelly had snuck out of the house to meet him. They were caught smoking weed and acting like they were on stronger stuff."

"Oh man. That's terrible."

"Yeah. Mel, my other sister, was there. She told me it was a train wreck. The hospital did toxicology tests and confirmed Mum's fears. The stable hand was fired."

"Drugs are bad news."

"They sure are. Not my thing." After Kelly's scary situation, Becky had stood firm and declined all offers of mind-altering substances. Her faith reinforced the wisdom of having self-control at all times. She didn't like eating junk, or ingesting junk in other ways.

He nodded. "It's a shame you lost the opportunity to go horse-back riding."

"It's okay. I was thirteen or fourteen and busy on weekends and during school holidays. Life goes on."

They rode in silence, their mounts content to stroll along the dirt road. It was dry, and the paddocks weren't as green as Becky had anticipated.

Sam opened a gate and Becky rode through, following Sam's lead.

"We'll be following this fence for a while," he said.

"What are you looking for?"

"Signs of damage."

"From what, exactly?" Her fence inspecting experience was zero.

"Deer. Elk."

"What about feral pigs?"

"You mean hogs, right?"

She nodded. "I know they're a problem in Australia."

"Fortunately wild hogs aren't common around these parts."

"That is fortunate." She felt safer knowing there weren't feral pigs roaming around.

"Have you made up your mind about the wedding?"

She nodded. "I'll be your plus-one."

His grin widened, highlighting a cute dimple near his mouth. "Thank you. I appreciate you doing this."

"No worries. Are you visiting here for Easter?"

"I sure am."

"Cindy wants to drive here on Easter Saturday. Can I catch a ride with you on Easter Sunday? I can stay at the dorm over the weekend."

"Sure. The cast and crew have an Easter Sunday wrap-up party. We can go there on the way."

"The party sounds fun."

"Have you received an email about your schedule?"

She nodded. "I'm volunteering in your area of expertise. I've never done this before, and I'll have no idea what I'm doing."

"It's easy once you learn the ropes. Same routine every perfor-mance. I'll see if we can be paired together."

"That would be fun. Then I'll know someone. I don't think any of my college friends are volunteering this year."

"No problem. I'm often paired with a newbie."

"Sounds good."

"Have you thought any more about switching churches?"

"Yeah. I think I'll stay where I am. Cindy's there, and a few girls I know from my dorm." She had reservations about the idea of people thinking they were in a relationship. Being friends was fine, but going to church with Sam felt more serious. People would notice and pair them together.

"If you change your mind, let me know. I can give you a ride there and back."

"I'll see how things pan out." A group of girls in her dorm from church met for a weekly Bible study. Once the play rehearsals started, she'd miss their evening gatherings, and the girls would miss the dinner Cindy and Becky prepared before the study. Cindy's semester schedule was busy, and the extra course load had chewed up her spare time. It would all work out. She looked forward to getting to know Sam as a friend.

"Have you seen the barn?" he asked.

"Not yet. Cindy mentioned that's where the family hold parties and celebrations."

"It's a fair size and has sentimental value. We sometimes use it to store hay bales."

"Is there hay in there now?"

He shook his head. "Aunt Lori insists that any hay stored in the barn is used first."

"That makes sense if the space is used for parties."

He nodded. "We're done checking fences."

"Did you find what you were looking for?"

"Fencing is fine. Good news. Why don't we stop by the barn on our way back to the stables?"

"Sure." She encouraged Caro into a trot and lengthened her stride into a canter, keeping pace with Sam and Beauty. She loved the feeling of the sun on her face and the wind in her hair. She'd forgotten how much she'd enjoyed riding.

The barn was a ten- or fifteen-minute walk from the homestead. The wooden structure stood tall on the flat plains, and it looked like it had an interesting history.

Sam tied up their horses and opened the barn door.

"Wow." She walked inside, impressed by the high beams and polished floorboards in the middle of the barn. Long tables were set up around the perimeter of the large space.

He smiled. "Uncle Joe and Aunt Lori restored it."

"They've done a great job." She walked through an open door on one side. "This space looks like it could be a commercial kitchen."

"It is. Aunt Lori insisted on a large area for catering purposes. They use the barn for larger family gatherings."

She headed back to the center of the barn, her footsteps loud on the floorboards. "Do you do line dancing?"

Sam nodded. "We grew up barn dancing. Only type of dancing I can do."

"I imagine you have great memories here."

"I do. Mom has a large extended family who still live around these parts."

"That's nice." She now understood the scope of Cindy's party planning with her mom. The ranch homestead was large, and the living room would be a tight fit for more than twenty people. The barn could seat a hundred or more, with a large dancing area in the middle. One day she'd love to attend a party held in the barn.

CHAPTER 6

Two weeks later, Sam smiled and nodded at the friendly faces in the Fount of Grace congregation as he moved along an aisle leading into the church foyer. The Sunday morning service had run over time. He was supposed to be arriving at his parents' home soon for lunch with Dad's family.

Sam had woken late and rushed to get ready for church. He'd forgotten to stow the specialist tools he needed for Dad's vintage Chevy in his truck. That would delay the start of his one-hour drive to visit his parents.

After lunch, when Dad's family left, Sam would spend a few hours working with Dad on the Chevy while Mom napped. He was worried about Mom. She worked long hours at the hospital and, in recent months, was more tired and exhausted during Sam's regular Sunday lunch visits.

He bonded with Dad over vintage vehicles, a constructive common interest that didn't bring them into conflict. Even on gloomy days, when it seemed like Dad's anxiety and depression was winning, the prospect of working on one of his prized cars with Sam could help motivate Dad to get out of bed and do something that brought him joy.

Sam was restoring a '68 Chevy that was garaged with his Cadillac Eldorado in a large shed in his back yard. He'd have less time to work on the Chevy now opening night was coming up. Rehearsals had already started, and he'd scheduled time to show Becky the ropes before their first full rehearsal.

Set moving was one of the easiest behind-the-scenes roles. The stage crew followed the same routine for each performance. They worked in pairs, or groups of four and six if they were moving larger props on and off the stage. Becky was smart, and she'd learn the routine by opening night.

Sam joined the coffee line. He needed more caffeine, and he'd take his coffee with him for the road. Small talk with acquaintances after the service was awkward and not his thing. Pete had quit inviting Sam out for lunch after church years ago. Sam had grown up with Sunday lunch being family time, and it was a habit he liked that had stuck firm.

If Sam was late for lunch, he'd add unnecessary stress to Mom's day. His parents were complicated. He hadn't realized how often he tiptoed on delicate eggshells around them until last year when they'd moved to another town.

Aunts, uncles, and cousins from Dad's side of the family would descend for lunch. Mom should say no sometimes. Dad's relatives had more time and energy than Mom to prepare lunch for a crowd. Dad didn't help Mom with lunch, either. The earlier Sam arrived for lunch, the less burden Mom carried on her already weighed-down shoulders.

"Hey, Sam."

He froze. Miley. He'd recognize her whiny nasal voice from the other side of the room. Except she wasn't across the room. She stood behind him in the line. He was cornered. Worst luck.

He half-turned toward her, his mouth set in a thin line. "Miley."

She giggled and curled a lock of blonde hair around her finger.

He glanced around the foyer. Where was Matt? When Sam had dated Miley in high school, he'd thought her hair curling move was cute. Now, he recognized it as a signal she wanted something.

"I heard you've RSVP'd a plus-one."

He nodded. He'd emailed Emma's family when he'd returned from the ranch. His initial relief that Becky had said yes had morphed into dread. Miley had an agenda, and he wasn't interested in engaging with her childish games.

"Who's this Becky girl?" Miley looked around. "Why isn't she at church with you?"

"Becky is Cindy's friend from college." Facts. Truth. Transparent honesty was his best option.

"She must go to church somewhere. You only date church girls."

Miley had been the only church girl he'd seriously dated. She'd strung him along for years in a long-distance relationship that had no future. He was the backup guy Miley had pulled out of her pocket when she needed him. During their relationship, her man radar had been on full beam, always scanning for a better offer. She'd found that better offer in Matt.

"What gives, Sam?" She batted her long and fake-looking eyelashes. "Cat got your tongue?"

He stared at the floor and moved a few steps forward in the line. The carpet needed cleaning. It looked like people spilled more coffee than they drank.

Could this line move any slower? He kept his focus on the front of the line. If he had the time, he'd pick up a coffee on his way out of town. Hightail it out of here, leaving Miley and this line in the dust.

He squared his shoulders, disappointed his cold shoulder hadn't given Miley the hint. He turned toward her, prepared for the inevitable verbal sparring. "She goes to Cindy's church."

"Oh, really? Pete made it sound like you and this Becky girl were almost engaged."

He gulped. What? Her red-tipped fingernail was on her mouth, dragging his gaze to her lips. No. He wasn't playing her game. She was married, and they were in church.

Miley had no shame. She could be making up stories to get information. He'd told Pete and the guys on Monday night that the blind date had gone well. They'd teased Sam about the date and his weekend away at the ranch. Guy talk was surface talk, and they had boundaries. They didn't talk about feelings like girls probably did.

He shrugged, trying to act nonchalantly while his mind raced for an appropriate response. "It's early days."

"This Becky girl really does exist."

He clenched his fists. "Of course." He turned his back on Miley and shuffled forward to the front of the line. How dare she accuse him of lying?

Guilty pinpricks pierced his conscience. He'd considered not correcting people who thought he and Becky were an item. He'd prayed about the Becky situation and changed his mind. Absolute honesty was the right choice.

Gilead was a small town with too many gossips. The sad truth was that even if he said he was only friends with Becky, the gossips like Mrs. Alleghany would run with their own version of events.

Miley refused to be ignored, stepping beside him and shoving her hands on her hips. "I want to meet her."

He widened his eyes. "You will. At Pete and Emma's wedding." Not a day sooner. Becky was nice. She didn't need to deal with Miley's inappropriate behavior.

"When I meet her, I'll know she's a real person."

He drew in a breath and focused on coffee, shutting Miley out, something he should have done years ago. Miley's snide remark didn't deserve an answer. It was Pete's words from

Monday night that lingered in his mind. According to Pete, the honeymoon phase of Matt and Miley's marriage had worn thin. Miley was trouble that Sam didn't want or need.

~

ON A CHILLY FIRST day of February, Becky's morning class finished and she shut down her laptop. Two hours disappeared fast when the teacher was entertaining and engaged their students in fruitful discussions. Her brain was full from taking notes and planning how to tackle her Old Testament history essay.

She placed her laptop in her oversized purse, ready for a relaxing one-hour lunch break. She'd arranged to meet Cindy in the cafeteria rather than trekking back to the dorm.

Becky stood and rolled her shoulders, feeling the kinks from slouching and sitting for too long. Maybe she should stop being lazy and drag herself to the gym on campus. Some core stretches might fix her posture.

Back in Sydney, she'd considered going to the gym a chore. The best part was catching up with friends in a coffee shop afterwards. She preferred her long and cold early morning walks to working out in the gym.

Corey, a guy she recognized from church, waved from across the room.

"Hey, Becky." He moved to her side. "How's things?"

"Busy." She shrugged on her coat, slung her purse over her shoulder, and walked with Corey to the door. "I'm trying to get ahead on my assignments before the passion play kicks off."

"Opening night is soon."

She nodded. "Only a few weeks away."

"It's an experience. The core group of volunteers work hard to pull it together. I volunteered last year. Highly recommend it. It's good for your resume, too."

She lengthened her strides in the hall, trying to ignore her hunger pangs. "My resume isn't a high priority."

He kept pace beside her. "Aren't you looking for ministry work?"

"I don't know. Maybe." That was the truth. When she returned to Australia in a few months, she'd pray and see what opportunities arose.

"Which king have you chosen for your essay?"

"David." They'd spent the morning studying 1 Kings, which confirmed her decision to write about David. She'd research the warrior king angle and focus on David's relationship with God.

"I'm going to write about Solomon and his wisdom."

"Okay." She exited the building and walked along the path toward the cafeteria. Corey stuck to her side like industrial-strength glue. Why? It was weird. Sometimes they'd chat for a few minutes when they ran into each other in classes and at church. This felt different.

"I have an idea," Corey said. "Why don't we work on King Solomon essays together?"

"Huh." She paused and shuffled to the edge of the wide walkway. Groups of people passed by. "Why would I do that?"

"Solomon will be easier than David. I can help you get a better grade."

She met his earnest gaze. "My grades are fine." She wasn't chasing high marks. Her goal was to learn more about the Bible and grow in her walk with Jesus. The essay question may be a better fit for Solomon. Whatever. She'd made up her mind.

He held her gaze. "It would be a better use of our time if we worked together. More efficient."

She broke eye contact, stepped off the path, and held her purse in both hands. Laptops were lighter now than when she was younger but were still heavy to lug around. "I'm good, Corey. Really." She wanted lunch more than she wanted to continue this conversation.

"King David will be a lot of work."

"I'm up for the challenge." She'd scheduled time to complete the assignment. Essay writing was one of her strengths.

"I can't change your mind…"

"No." She shook her head. "I'm not interested in researching Solomon."

"May I ask why?"

Oh boy. This wasn't going to end well. "You really want to know?"

"I'm curious, so yes."

She tapped her foot. "We can walk and talk. I'm meeting Cindy at the cafeteria in a few minutes."

"Sure." He fell back into step beside her.

Where to start? "How many wives and concubines did Solomon have?"

"Let me think. Seven hundred wives and three hundred concubines."

"That's right." Corey was a walking Bible encyclopedia. During class discussions he was one of those people who contributed all the right answers. "I find those numbers disconcerting."

"They're facts." A determined tone filled his voice.

She frowned and lengthened her stride. "I'm not disputing Bible facts." If she wasn't hungry and meeting Cindy, she'd go power walking in the opposite direction to Corey. "I don't want to write an essay on a man like Solomon."

"The women were from foreign treaty deals."

"That's what I don't like." The cafeteria entrance was up ahead. Where was Cindy? "We're talking about a powerful man. A king who treated women like property." A king who potentially had intimate relationships with a thousand women. Blech.

"The women aren't the focus of the essay question. Life was different in the ancient world. King Solomon's marriages were strategic political alliances."

"I'm aware of that." She couldn't shrug this off as an inconsequential detail. "We're talking about a thousand women, Corey. Hundreds of wives. Can you imagine anyone in twenty-first century Christian circles thinking that was okay?"

"Obviously not, but Solomon was renowned for his wisdom."

"True, but from my perspective the man had a lust problem."

"I don't follow. Why's that relevant?" He sounded genuinely puzzled.

"I get that Solomon gained wealth and power from the marriages. But it's a far cry from our modern-day Biblical interpretation of marriage."

"You're comparing apples with oranges, Becky. It was a different culture. A different world."

"Maybe. But I struggle to understand how a man gifted with wisdom from God could think a palace harem was a good idea." No one was perfect. Everyone struggled with temptation in different areas of their lives. She didn't want to research Solomon and have to reconcile his wisdom with his hedonistic lifestyle choices.

"If we're talking about morals, then his father wasn't a poster boy for good behavior. David had half a dozen wives and he committed adultery."

"That's fair. David wasn't a saint. But there were consequences from his actions with Bathsheba."

Corey nodded. "They paid a big price."

"They sure did." The Bathsheba situation would fall outside the scope of the essay question. David and Bathsheba had been punished by God. Their baby died. Becky couldn't imagine how painful it would have been to walk in their shoes. Despite his wisdom, Solomon made his share of mistakes. His foreign wives led him astray and encouraged him to worship their gods.

"Becky." Cindy waved and met them at the cafeteria entrance. "Let's join the line before it gets too long."

Corey cleared his throat. "Can I join you for lunch?"

"Sure." She followed Cindy and Corey indoors and they stood in line.

"How was class?" Cindy asked.

Becky smiled. "It was fascinating. We're looking at 1 Kings. I'm going to search for fiction set during that time period."

Corey raised an eyebrow. "Why fiction? You need nonfiction with facts. Fiction is useless for research purposes."

"I like reading historical fiction. If the author has done their research, then I'm intrigued by their insights into culture and the lives of the people."

"It's not a good idea to read fiction," he said.

Cindy's eyebrows shot up. She stayed silent, seemingly content to listen.

"Why?" A sinking feeling filled her mind. "It's Biblical fiction that reflects God's truth. I like Christian fiction set during the Roman era as well."

He shook his head. "Fiction is stories. It's not truth. It could lead you astray."

Wait a minute. Did Corey think it was wrong to read any fiction? "Do you read fiction?"

He shook his head vigorously. "Never. It's not good for you."

"It's entertainment that reflects Christian values. More wholesome than most TV shows and movies."

"Becky, I urge you to think more on this. Is it edifying to consume made-up stories?"

"Jesus told stories and parables. He didn't have a problem with using fiction to illustrate a point."

"Jesus is different. He's the way, the truth, and the life. Everything He spoke was truth. Fiction is not truth."

Oh boy. She was on a losing ticket to nowhere if she continued this conversation. "I have a different perspective."

Corey nodded. "I'll be praying for you."

His sincerity was commendable, but his prayers wouldn't change her mind. "That's thoughtful of you."

"What did you two discuss in class?" Cindy moved them forward in the line and moved their conversation onto neutral ground.

She shuffled forward, her gaze drawn to the lunch menu. "Israel and the kings."

"Sounds interesting," Cindy said.

"We also discussed our essay topic," Corey said.

"Are you doing the same topic?" Cindy asked.

"No. We have very different ideas." That conversation topic was closed. Becky had no interest in revisiting Corey's thoughts on Solomon and wisdom.

"I'd like to talk more." Corey turned to face her. "Would you like to discuss our essays over lunch on Sunday after church? Pick your restaurant. I'm not fussy with food."

Cindy looked like she'd choked on her words, suppressing a snicker. "Becky is fussy, so…"

"Actually, Corey, thanks for asking but I can't."

"We could make it the following Sunday."

Becky met Cindy's wide-eyed gaze. The penny dropped, like a piece of metal clanging on concrete flooring. Corey was interested in dating her. Duh. It explained a lot.

"Becky is thinking about changing churches," Cindy said.

He stepped closer to Becky. "Why? Did something happen? You've been a regular since classes started in the fall."

She swallowed a groan and a gallon of courage. He was looking for a wife. A wife who didn't read fiction. Why couldn't he see that she wasn't a suitable candidate?

"What do you say, Becky? Is it a date?"

She switched her purse to the other shoulder. "I'm moving home to Australia in a few months."

He smiled. "I'm praying about overseas mission opportunities. Australia would work."

What? No. "I'm sorry, Corey. I'm changing churches because I've met someone. I probably won't be returning to your church."

His expression dimmed, the light fading in his eyes. "I had no idea. I hadn't seen you with anyone and assumed…"

"That's fair. It's early days, and I don't like to rush into things." The old Bek dived in headfirst. The new Becky exercised caution and considered options.

"Yeah, I get it. Can we still have lunch today? Now we're lined up together and all."

She nodded. "Sure. We can be friends."

"Good. If things don't work out…"

Ugh. She'd said the wrong thing. He'd taken her response as a sign of hope.

Cindy jumped in, taking control. "What's the lunch special? I feel like chicken."

Corey switched gears to the lunch menu topic, and Becky let out a long breath. She'd done it now. Sam was stuck with her attending his church, whether he still liked that idea or not. If she stayed at her current church, Corey would consider her fair game and on the market for a husband. She didn't want to hurt Corey's feelings if it could be avoided.

The first Saturday full rehearsal with the cast and crew was coming up this weekend. She'd talk to Sam about going to church with him on Sunday morning — assuming Cindy didn't get in first. She wouldn't put it past Cindy to send a sneaky text to her cousin during lunch.

Becky had agreed to be Sam's plus-one. She'd make the switch to Sam's church. The Gilead townsfolk would add two plus two and come up with five. It was game on for the fake relationship. Rumors of her supposed romance with Sam would circulate around town. The upside was she liked Sam, and their attraction was real. She wouldn't be faking any tingles, and it wouldn't be a hardship to spend more time with Sam.

CHAPTER 7

Sam arrived at the auditorium early on Saturday morning and greeted the busy volunteers preparing for the rehearsal. Excitement hummed in the air, accompanied by the musicians who were warming up in the orchestra pit. Today was a full rehearsal, and the first time he'd work through all the sequential set changes with Becky. She was a fast learner and followed instructions, which made his job easier.

He wandered around backstage, checking all his props were in place. The props didn't change from year to year. He'd been assigned his usual role on stage crew, a role he could do without looking at the script or a run sheet.

They'd completed a comprehensive safety audit during the auditions. Broken or damaged props, or props that were showing their age had been identified and either repaired or replaced. He confirmed the sturdiness of the tables and chairs. Wobbly legs were a hazard they checked on a regular basis.

Becky joined him backstage. "Hey Sam, do we have time for coffee?"

"We do if we're quick." He walked with her to the stage, pausing to secure a tiny section of tape over one of the leads. It looked like something heavy had been dragged over the cord. He'd keep an eye open for trip hazards. During the week he'd met Dawson, the new guy from the college who was taking care of AV. Sam was impressed by Dawson's attention to detail.

"A small coffee is all I need." Becky fell into step beside him.

"That's good. We're only allowed bottled water backstage."

She met his gaze, her smile wide. "That works."

Her vibrant smile set off cartwheels in his stomach. *Get a grip, Sam.* He was here to do a job, not daydream about Becky's smile. He should be used to her smile by now. He should have immunity from the charming way her smile lit up her beautiful blue eyes.

Focus. Think about coffee. Letty had set up refreshment tables at the back of the auditorium.

He followed Becky down the steps at the side of the stage and into a clear aisle. Groups of people had gathered in the auditorium, including the extras who participated in the crowd scenes. Becky could have received the same college credits from being an extra. Stage crew was hard work by comparison.

They collected two small cups of coffee. He added sugar.

Becky sipped her black coffee. "I needed this."

"It'll keep us going until lunch."

She nodded at the people lingering in the auditorium. "There are so many people here."

"Friends and family are invited to the rehearsals."

"I'd forgotten about that."

"We have spectators who watch all the auditions."

"I didn't know that was a thing."

"It is in Gilead." Sam would rather have a tooth pulled than sit through hours of cringeworthy auditions. He'd caught enough of the auditions during his brief visits with the stage crew to look at the props.

Many of the Gilead townsfolk lacked serious talent. They turned up year after year, performing the same old and worn-out audition pieces. Sam assumed they all shared in the vain hope that they'd land a bigger role than crowd scenes.

Becky opened her purse. A wad of papers were rolled up like a scroll. "I might need to refer to this."

He chuckled. "You won't need it."

"Just in case. What if something happened to you?"

"One of the other teams would take over and help out."

"Okay." She pressed her lips together. "This play is important, and I don't want to mess it up."

"I can give you one foolproof tip."

She quirked an eyebrow. "Which is?"

"Don't sneak food or drink backstage."

"Huh. Did someone really do that?"

He nodded. "A few years ago. College student. She snuck muffins from Letty's table, hid them backstage, and snacked during rehearsal."

"Oh." She pointed at Letty's plates of muffins on the table. "They're divine, but hiding them backstage…"

"Yup. It was wild. The crumb trail gave the game away."

"What happened to her?"

"She was caught red-handed and quit on the spot."

"Wow. Then you were short of volunteers."

"We had it covered." He grinned. "Her replacement didn't have an out-of-control addiction to Letty's delicious muffins."

She chuckled. "I'm glad it worked out. I'm still worried I'll forget something important."

"We'll be fine. Don't forget the visual prop cues on the stage. We'll take the same items on and off stage. I've lined the props up in rotation order, and we only work from one side of the stage." More set-moving activity happened from the back and the opposite side of the stage. Sam's familiarity with stage crew work was why they paired him with newbie volunteers.

She nodded. "Will the rehearsal take long?"

"It depends."

"I hope it runs smoothly today." She finished her coffee. "Please excuse me. I'll visit the restroom before we start."

"Good idea."

Becky headed for an exit. She passed Connor, who was walking in the opposite direction. Sam returned Connor's smile and wave. The guy was hard to recognize, decked out in his Jesus costume. Did Connor know today's rehearsal wasn't a dress rehearsal?

Connor had shared his disappointment in missing out on playing Judas. A guy called Leo, who Sam didn't know, had picked up the Judas role.

Sam stretched out his hand toward Connor. "I've always wanted to shake hands with Jesus."

"Ha-ha." Connor shook Sam's hand. "I'm the imposter who's pretending to know what I'm doing."

"No way. I've seen you rehearse. You know your stuff. The Jesus role suits you." Connor had talent, and Sam understood why they'd cast him in the larger role of Jesus.

"I'm not so sure. They made a casting mistake. Mixed up the names, or something."

Sam placed a reassuring hand on Connor's shoulder. "You'll be fine. I'm praying for you."

Connor's eyebrows shot up. "Whoa. You don't need to do that."

"I do." Sam held Connor's gaze. "You have this role for a reason. I'm praying you'll work out that reason soon."

"It won't be today. I'm too nervous."

Sam shook his head. "Break a leg or something. Broken bones are the only way out of playing the role."

"I'm not breaking any bones. But I'll take all the luck I can find."

"You won't need luck. You've got this, Connor."

Connor nodded. "See you backstage."

"You sure will." God had plans for Connor. Each year Sam

prayed daily for someone involved in the play during the lead-up to Easter. This year God had put Connor's name on his heart. He'd keep on praying for Connor, praying for opportunities for Sam and others to talk to Connor about Jesus. There was no passion play without Jesus, and Connor was perfect for the role.

AFTER LUNCH, Becky stood at the side of the stage, fascinated by the rehearsal. The passion play was a professional performance. She understood why people traveled interstate to see it. She loved having a close-up behind-the-scenes view of the rehearsal.

Becky could feel every inch of the soles of her feet. She'd worn sneakers for the full rehearsal, knowing she'd clock up the steps. Her sensible footwear hadn't made a difference. She'd lost all her endurance for being on her feet all day. Back in high school, she'd worked long shifts in retail without pain. Her stamina was gone. The gym beckoned.

She'd rather take a seat than go to the gym. Seats were available backstage, and there was time between set changes to sit and rest her feet.

Sam was smart. He'd paced himself and spent most of his time backstage with the crew. Sam had introduced her to so many people that she'd lost track of all their names. They were a friendly bunch, and Becky was glad she'd volunteered for stage crew.

She'd spent most of her day standing in the wings, her attention riveted on the action unfolding on the stage. The star of the show was a new guy who was friends with Sam. Connor was dressed as Jesus, even though the other actors wore street clothes. Connor had said the costume helped him get into character. Becky couldn't argue with his logic. Connor's performance was flawless.

Most of the set-changing activity happened from the back

and other side of the stage. The actors usually waited in the wings near her and Sam. She'd heard about the famous John Johnson, who'd walked the floorboards in this auditorium, and was discovered in Gilead by a talent scout.

The actors took a break and she peeked around the curtains. The auditorium was a quarter full. Letty's refreshment tables from lunch were almost empty. Her coffee, and the high energy levels in the auditorium, had kept Becky going.

Leo, the young guy who'd scored the role of Judas, headed her way. He'd spent half the day talking to her. Leo claimed he was in love with her accent, which was ridiculous.

"Becky, you're our most devoted fan." Leo's enthusiasm for the play was contagious.

She laughed. "Alice may argue that point." Leo's fiancée, who Becky knew from college classes, was an extra in the crowd scenes.

"Alice won't mind. Do you have plans tomorrow? Alice said you liked horseback riding. We're spending the day with her folks at their farm."

Three was a crowd. Alice had shared this morning how much she looked forward to uninterrupted time with Leo tomorrow. He was like an Energizer bunny who kept on going and didn't have an off button.

"I'll pass, Leo. I've church in the morning."

"You could skip this week."

She shook her head. "I can't, sorry. You'll enjoy a day out with Alice."

"I'll miss your sweet Aussie voice."

He was a charmer. "You'll cope." Alice had an acre of patience in dealing with her fun and flirty fiancé. Leo was an extrovert who could talk to anyone. Anywhere. Anytime. "You'll see me all the time when the play opens."

"True. True. We'll be living in this auditorium." He paused, listening to the loudspeaker announcement. "Time to go back onstage and kill myself. Again."

She snickered. "You're too happy to play Judas."

"You'll see the depths of my despair. Ciao."

She shook her head. Leo was hilarious. The next act was a short scene called The Despair of Judas. How Leo could flip a switch and move like lightning into tormented Judas's headspace was beyond her comprehension. The orchestra set the tone with dramatic musical backdrops.

Sam appeared by her side. "We're back on in five. We'll move the plants onstage for the next act with Pilate."

"No problem." The fake potted plants were featured in multiple acts. Her job, when the current scene ended, was to remove the stool Judas used to hang himself. A morbid thought.

She'd picked up the rhythm of the rehearsal schedule. It was one thing to see individual acts during various rehearsals, but it was nothing like watching the acts pulled together in sequential order. She was intrigued by the thought of seeing real donkeys playing their part in the play.

Sam was right. She could ditch the script notes and follow along with his clever prop rotation system. It helped that they moved the smaller props, including chairs and tables. She was impressed by the efficiency and speed of the set changes made by the crew.

Her feet were sore, but she stayed near the stage, following the play, entranced by the action taking place. Powerful. Compelling. Spellbinding. Jesus's suffering was greater than her minor issue with sore feet. His feet were pierced for her transgressions. His body nailed to a cross. The emotional rollercoaster was exhilarating and exhausting.

Sam was by her side for the final acts. They watched in silence. The second to last act broke open her floodgates. Tears streaked her cheeks. Too many tears to wipe away with the back of her hand and hide the evidence.

The joy in the final act was a gentle balm for her soul. *He is risen.* That phrase had a deeper meaning now she'd seen the barbaric actions that led to His death played out in front of her eyes. This was only the rehearsal, and she felt like she'd gone a few rounds in an emotional wringer.

The curtains closed on the final act and she let out a long and heartfelt sigh. Wow. If only she'd visited the Bavarian town of Oberammergau during their once-a-decade passion play season. The passion play in an outdoor theater would be amazing to watch, even though her German was rusty.

Sam placed his hand on her forearm. "Are you okay?"

"Yeah." She sniffled and wiped the back of her hand across her eyes. "It's intense."

"Wait until opening night. The atmosphere with a full house is out of this world."

"I can only imagine." She helped Sam move the props backstage and out of the way. They wouldn't have exclusive use of the college auditorium until opening night. "Sam, about church. Are you going to your church tomorrow morning?"

He nodded. "Have you changed your mind?"

"I have, actually. I'd love to visit your church tomorrow."

"That will work." He paused. His gaze drilled into her, seeking answers. "Why the change of heart?"

"There was a situation. Last week at college."

"This doesn't sound good."

"Put it this way." He didn't need to know the ins and outs of why she'd changed her mind. "It would help me if we were seen around town together."

His eyebrows lifted. "Are you saying you want to do the fake relationship?"

"Sort of. Not really. I don't know."

"I have my reservations, too."

"It can't hurt for us to be friends who spend a lot of time together. People will draw their own conclusions."

"That they will." Sam turned to her. "Do you have dinner plans?"

She shook her head. "Cindy's at the ranch. I was going to microwave something easy from the freezer."

"From your supply of precooked meals."

"Yeah. Cindy will restock our freezer tomorrow."

"Do you feel like pizza? The pizzeria in town is good, and they have dine-in options."

"That works."

He smiled. "Okay. Let's get out of here. I'm starving."

"Me too." She grabbed her coat and purse. "We'll need to have our own pizzas. A small will do me."

"Sure. I always order the meatlovers."

"Always."

"Yeah. Pepperoni. Sausage. Ham. Bacon. Meatballs. Extra cheese."

"That's a lot of meat."

"You should try it."

"Not my thing." They exited the auditorium. The chilly breeze whipped around her face. She retrieved her woolen scarf from her coat pocket and wound it around her neck.

"Are you ordering vegan?" he asked.

"No. I'll create my own topping combo. Vegetables with pineapple."

He stopped and turned to stare at her. "Pineapple on pizza. With vegetables."

"Yeah. Plus mozzarella cheese."

"Pineapple doesn't belong on pizza."

She snickered. "It does in Australia."

"What about ham? Wouldn't you at least eat ham and pineapple together?"

"Sorry. I'm not a Hawaiian pizza fan."

He shook his head. "I don't understand you and your food choices."

"You eat grits for breakfast. That's plain weird."

"Have you tried homemade grits?"

She scrunched her nose. "They are wrong. More wrong than pineapple on pizza."

"I disagree. Grits are traditional Southern food."

"People around the world eat pineapple on pizza. I haven't seen grits on a breakfast menu in Australia."

"That's not the point." He walked beside her on the sidewalk. "Do you always have to win an argument?"

"Nope. But I do if I'm right." She pulled her scarf higher over the back of her head. "I'll apologize if I'm wrong."

"That's fair."

"I have a question. What are your thoughts on reading fiction?"

He shot her a quizzical look. "That's a bit random."

"I had a conversation with someone at college that thankfully didn't turn into an argument." Becky had held back, exerting self-control to ensure she didn't say something to Corey that she'd later regret.

"I'm not a big reader. I haven't read a novel this year."

"That's okay." It was only February. He had plenty of months left in the year for reading. That was if he wanted to read. "Do you have a problem with other people reading fiction?"

"Why would I care?"

"Good point." She appreciated his logic and understanding of boundaries. Corey could learn a thing or two from Sam. "I was told I should stop reading Christian fiction because it's not edifying."

"What? Someone said that?"

"They sure did." Sam didn't need to know about the other stuff Corey had said. "Cindy changed the subject before the conversation could turn into an argument."

"Is this what you talk about at Bible college?"

"Not usually. What are your thoughts on Christian fiction?"

He smiled. "Mom loves reading it. She works in a hospital and likes reading romances set there."

"You mean contemporary romance with medical themes? I like those, too."

"Yeah, I guess. I buy Mom books for birthdays and Christmas. There's an author she likes with hospital books. Her name is Heather something. I think it's a color."

"Her last name is a color."

He nodded. "Brown. White. Black. Green. No, it's gray. Heather Gray."

"I'll have to look her up."

"Mom raves about her. The paperbacks are on her bookshelf."

"Sounds fun." Her foot caught on something and she fell forward.

Strong arms encircled her, preventing her nose from crash-landing on the sidewalk. Or something worse. Fractured bones, or broken teeth requiring a visit to the dentist. Her problem molar was now fixed, and she was free of tooth pain.

She leaned back into his chest, steadying her aching feet. It felt good being in his arms. Too good. He'd saved her from a trip to the ER.

She turned in his arms, facing him. Eyes locked on his. The atmosphere was charged with sparks warmer than crackling wood in an indoor fireplace.

She stared at his lips, wondering what it would be like to kiss him.

His hand cupped her cheek. "Becky —"

"Look at you two."

Mrs. Alleghany's triumphant voice brought her back to reality.

"Don't let me interrupt your moment." The gleam in Mrs. Alleghany's eyes made it clear she knew exactly what she'd interrupted.

Sam stepped to the side, one arm secured around her waist. "We won't. Enjoy your evening."

Mrs. Alleghany passed by and Becky fell into step beside Sam. She appreciated his arm circling her waist. Her aching feet needed a long rest at the pizzeria. Mrs. Alleghany would tell the whole town an exaggerated version of what she'd witnessed by morning. Becky accompanying Sam to church tomorrow morning would confirm the truth in Mrs. Alleghany's gossip.

Sam cleared his throat. "Are your feet okay?"

"Yeah. Just sore from standing too much."

"Not far to walk now. It looks like our fake relationship is on. The gossip will spread fast."

"We could deny it. But no one will believe us."

"So we say nothing. Do our own thing and ignore the speculation. Let people draw their own conclusions."

Sam's protective arm around her was sensible. And nice. He smelled good. A woodsy scent that suited him. He was looking way too attractive. She wasn't faking how his close proximity affected her. Oh boy, were they heading for trouble?

CHAPTER 8

A week later, Becky stood in the back of the auditorium, waiting for the dress rehearsal to start. She sipped her morning coffee and soaked in the atmosphere. The actors were in costume, and it was like she'd traveled back in time to the ancient world. Connor stood out in the crowd. She'd recognize his distinctive Jesus costume from a mile away.

Sam had drunk his coffee fast. They'd needed his help backstage to fix something. She'd learned Sam's farm mechanic skills were transferable to other things, including stage props and vintage cars. Dad would love to talk cars with Sam. During her family video call last week, she'd heard all about Dad's latest vintage Jaguar purchase.

Sam had introduced her to Noah, who was playing one of the centurion roles. Noah's costume was impressive, and he'd given her the scoop on the petting zoo. She hadn't considered the logistics of donkeys performing in the play and where they'd be accommodated. A petting zoo would be set up near the auditorium as a tourist attraction for the kids. It sounded like a lot of fun.

Becky checked the time on her phone and snagged an apple

spice muffin. Alice joined her by the table, black coffee in hand, her cheerful face marred by fatigue lines.

"How's Leo doing?" Becky asked.

"He's struggling on." Alice sipped her coffee. "Very disappointed he had to pull out of the play."

"I'm sorry." Poor Leo had broken his leg in a horse-riding accident last weekend.

"He's still at the farm. Mom said he's a handful and not the best-behaved patient."

She held back a snicker. "That doesn't surprise me."

"Yeah." Alice sighed. "We might need to delay our wedding."

"Oh, Alice. That's not good news."

She nodded. "It's one reason why we're not sharing the accident details. People hear broken leg and panic. We don't want to postpone if we can avoid it."

"That's understandable." Wedding planning was stressful enough without the added complication of broken bones.

"Have you met the new guy who's playing Judas?" Alice asked.

"Not yet."

"I've heard he's good looking."

"Same. He's the hot conversation topic." Miles Davies. The mystery man. He hadn't attended any of the auditions yet had somehow scored a plum role.

Alice lifted her brows. "You know there's more than one hot topic of conversation happening today."

"Oh, really. This town talks too much." She should be used to small-town gossip by now.

"You're not wrong. They're talking about you."

Her mouth fell open. "What? Me? Who would care?"

"Mrs. Alleghany. She claims she caught you and Sam smooching on Main Street after the rehearsal last week."

Her cheeks heated. "Mrs. Alleghany has misinterpreted the situation. I tripped over and Sam caught me. No big deal."

Alice laughed. "If I didn't have Leo, I wouldn't mind being rescued by Sam. It sounds romantic, Becky."

"It's not. Really."

"Honey, you keep on telling yourself that. Sam's a good guy. Loyal. Reliable. A keeper. Think about it." She finished her coffee. "I have to go. See you at lunch."

"For sure." It was nice having Alice around to hang out with during their breaks. Especially now she and Sam were on the gossip radar.

Alice headed over to the seating area where groups of extras congregated.

The heat in Becky's face cooled back to normal temperature. If she kept blushing at the mention of Sam and the Main Street mishap, the town would have them married by Easter.

She walked around to backstage, doing her best to avoid eye contact with anyone who might ask intrusive questions. Mrs. Alleghany had good intentions, but her penchant for salivating over juicy gossip was well known in Gilead. At least the stories about her and Sam would soon become old news, just as soon as someone else caught Mrs. Alleghany's attention.

Becky spotted Sam in their prop area beside the stage, chatting with one of the actors. She should check in and find out what needed to be done before the first act.

She hesitated. Alice had homed in on the truth. There was something going on between her and Sam. Something that wasn't a fake relationship. They'd almost kissed last weekend.

But it didn't matter if people talked, or didn't talk, about them. Today they had a job to do. She waved at Sam, snagging his attention and he signaled for her to come on over. The actor had his back facing her. Today had started well, despite Mrs. Alleghany's gossip. Another sore feet day was on the cards, but it would be worth it to see the actors perform the full dress rehearsal.

"Hey, Sam." She smiled and played it cool. The town gossips didn't need any more fuel to burn.

His smile lit up his eyes, a deep blue that matched his shirt. "Becky. Have you met Miles? He's our new Judas."

She turned to Miles. Her smile faltered. Her face heated. Her heart pounded. No. She must be mistaken.

Miles's gaze locked on hers. The slight widening of his eyes was the only indication he'd recognized her. "Nice to meet you. Becky."

"Same." Oh boy. That voice. The way he'd spoken her name confirmed her fears. She wrenched her gaze away from Miles's familiar face and glanced over Sam's shoulder. "I'll visit the restroom. Be back soon."

"No worries," Sam said.

She took slow and even steps, resisting the temptation to run. What was Logan Miles doing in Gilead? His long brown hair and hipster beard was a good disguise. In his recent action movies, he'd sported shorter blond hair and no beard. His blue eyes were the same, but he was leaner in build. His costume and disguise would fool people who'd never met the famous Hollywood actor in person. Becky wasn't one of those people.

She joined the restroom line, happy it was a long line. She needed thinking time. Time to regain her composure. Logan Miles was a connection to Jarrod and her past that could unravel her plans to continue hiding in Gilead. Only a small group of trusted friends and family back home knew her exact location. She'd shut down all her social media accounts, telling the world she was taking a year off to travel and explore the world.

Breath in. Breathe out. Don't panic.

The mantra she repeated, interspersed with desperate prayers. Out of all the Hollywood actors, why was Logan Miles the one who'd landed in Gilead? Australia was a large country, and Logan had only filmed one movie there. Becky wasn't an actor and wasn't involved in the film industry. No one should make the connection and guess she'd met Logan before he arrived in Gilead.

She returned to her usual position at the side of the stage, thankful Logan had gone someplace else. Miles. She had to think of him as Miles and call him Miles. He must have his own reasons for hiding his identity.

The rehearsal started. Becky was glad the crew expected her to watch from the wings. Less chance of falling into an awkward group conversation with Logan Miles. She could keep to herself, focus on the performance, and forget that her past had caught up with her like a terrifying tornado tearing through town.

Logan Miles was a true talent. His voice was unrecognizable as he embraced the role of Judas and made it his own. They took a break for lunch, and Logan disappeared.

She ate her lunch in the break area with Alice and her friends from the cast. Their lunch chatter included comments on how Miles was reclusive and didn't mingle with anyone. Becky nodded and kept her mouth shut.

With time to spare after she finished her lunch, she made her excuses and found a seat in a cozy corner of the backstage area.

Sam pulled up chair beside her. "You're quiet today."

Ugh. He'd noticed something was off. "I'm a bit tired. Stayed up late last night to get a head start on an assignment." That was the truth. She'd felt like having two coffees this morning.

"How's school going?" Concern infused his voice.

"Good." She stared into his eyes and blocked out the backstage activity buzzing around them. "I'm keeping up and planning how to manage my studies around the play."

"It's a juggling act." He paused, his knee close to hers. "I'm guessing you've heard the gossip about us."

She nodded. "It's not unexpected." If only gossip was her biggest problem. She resisted the temptation to place her hand on his knee. He was solid and steady, like a lighthouse on a headland. She was thrashing around in the ocean in an inflatable lifeboat, feeling like her world was topsy-turvy and at risk of falling apart.

"I'm sorry it's bothering you."

Her heart skipped ahead to a new up-tempo beat. Sam was a sweet guy. He was concerned about her feelings. "I'll be okay."

"Don't let it get you down."

"I won't." Had he picked up on her reaction to Logan and thought it related to gossip? "We've discussed how we'll both benefit from people thinking we're together."

"Are you sure?"

"I'm sure. It'll all work out." Somehow. If she could avoid Logan Miles and act normal when he was around, then no one needed to discover their Australian connection. It's not like she'd dated Logan. Sure, the Australian paparazzi had published photos of them, but Jarrod had always been in the pictures. Jarrod was the connection she wanted to stay buried.

When their break was over, she and Sam moved to their position near the stage for the afternoon rehearsal. It was fun seeing how different the cast looked in their costumes. Some people she recognized, while others looked and sounded nothing like their real selves.

She succeeded in avoiding Logan Miles until the end of his last act on stage. She retrieved the Judas stool and Logan followed her to her usual spot in the wings.

"Bek, we need to talk. But not here."

She nodded. "Where?" It was inevitable. She was thankful he wasn't blowing her cover.

"I'll be here when you finish setting up the next scene."

"Okay." She rotated the props on autopilot, glad she'd paid attention to the routine last week. She'd attract Sam's attention if she messed up the props.

Sam headed backstage and she returned to her usual position.

Logan stepped in front of her, blocking her view of the stage. "Do you have your phone?"

She nodded. He was serious about wanting to talk. Why?

"Look like you're checking something on your phone, then hand it to me. I'll add my number and send myself a message."

"I can do that." She pulled her phone out of her pocket and unlocked the screen. The next act started, and the people nearby swung their attention to the stage.

She placed her phone in Logan's palm. Millions of girls would love to be in her situation, exchanging phone numbers with Logan. All she could feel was dread. She didn't want anyone noticing their interaction.

Minutes later he reached for her hand and placed her phone on her palm.

"You're B and I'm L."

"Huh."

"That's our code. For our names. In case someone sees a message."

"Got it." Why did she feel like she'd been cast in a lead role in a spy novel?

"I'll be in touch tomorrow."

"Okay."

"Does anyone in Gilead call you Bek?"

"No." Except for Letty and her crew, who sometimes shortened her name when writing on her coffee cup. That didn't count, right?

He nodded. "Take care of yourself."

Logan disappeared backstage and she pocketed her phone, switching her attention to the stage.

What had just happened? She was now taking part in clandestine meetings with Logan Miles. Could her life get any weirder?

THE NEXT DAY, Sam and Becky left their church building after the morning service and walked together toward Sam's truck. Sam's plan was to collect Cindy from her church on their way to Mom and Dad's for lunch.

After the rehearsal yesterday, Becky had accepted his invitation to join him for dinner at the pizzeria. Cindy had tagged along, and they'd shared a nice dinner. They'd made arrangements to travel to his parents' home for lunch. Mom was keen to catch up with Cindy and meet Becky.

Becky hopped into the passenger seat of his truck and secured her seatbelt. "I like your church."

"I'm glad. It's you're church now."

"Not for long. I'm heading home in June."

He switched on the engine, and the reality of her words sank in. This friendship, this thing happening between them, had an expiry date. He wasn't sure how he felt about that. He drove along Main Street, passing familiar landmarks. He had an expiry date on attending his church in Gilead, too.

He pulled into a parking space around the corner from Cindy's church. They had a few minutes before the service would end.

Becky turned toward him. "Please tell me about your parents. What do I need to know?"

He lowered his window a few inches. "Mom is great. You'll like her. She's heard glowing things about you from my family at the ranch."

"Okay. And your dad. What's he like?"

He blew out a long breath. "Dad is more complicated. He was badly injured in a mill accident when I was kid."

"I'm sorry." Her voice softened and she shifted in her seat, meeting his gaze. "Did he recover from his injuries?"

"Physically, yes. He's had a lifelong struggle with depression and anxiety."

"That's hard."

He nodded. The burden of Dad's mental health issues had fallen on Mom's weary shoulders. "We lived at the ranch for a few years after his accident. Aunt Lori homeschooled me with my cousins while Mom worked as a nurse."

"That makes sense. I'd wondered if you'd lived at the ranch."

"The ranch is my home." He might as well share his plans with her. Better for Becky to hear them from him than from his parents. "I'd like to move there later this year."

Her eyes widened. "Oh, wow. You're leaving Gilead."

"That's the plan. Time for a change and all that. Not many people know."

She nodded. "My lips are sealed. It's an exciting move for you. Will you still work as a farm mechanic?"

"Probably." One of the many details he'd need to iron out. "I'd base myself at the ranch and see if there's work available."

"This might be your last year volunteering for the play."

"Yup." He'd helped with the crew for seven years in a row. He'd keep his Colorado plans under wraps until they were set in stone.

"They'll miss you."

"I can drive back at Easter and watch the play."

"True." She smiled. "I don't regret volunteering."

He nodded. The play was the connection that had drawn them together. Becky was diligent and hard working. She took her volunteer role seriously, and he could count on her. That meant a lot. An attractive trait that made the prospect of kissing her more appealing. He shouldn't be thinking about kissing her. Except they were alone in his truck, and he was drawn to her like an invisible magnet, an undeniable attraction he tried to put out of his mind.

Cindy waved and settled in the back seat. They made good time in driving to his parents. The girls talked and talked, and he was content to listen. Cindy had brought along a cloth bag full of books for Mom that she'd collected from the ranch. Their mothers swapped paperbacks on a regular basis, using Cindy as their free carrier pigeon.

He pulled into the driveway behind Mom's hatchback. The girls went indoors ahead of him, and he unpacked his tools. Dad hadn't opened up the garage at the back. Was he having a bad day and still in bed? Sometimes Dad struggled to get up and moving until early afternoon or later. Dad usually made an effort on Sundays, despite having a list of excuses longer than the road from Gilead to avoid attending Sunday morning church with Mom.

Sam carried his toolbox around the back to the deck. Mom had fired up the grill. Burgers were probably on the menu. He hoped Cindy had warned Mom that Becky was fussy with food. Last night, Becky had ordered pizza with spinach on it. Green stuff on pizza was wrong, but they'd agreed to disagree. Again.

"Sam." Mom walked into his arms and hugged him close. "It's so good to see you."

"You too. Love you, Mom." She looked more tired than usual. He was worried about her. She worked too much.

"Love you too, son." She stepped back, her gaze sweeping over him. "I like your Becky."

"She's not my Becky."

"That's not what Lori said."

"We're friends, Mom. It was Cindy's idea for Becky to join us for lunch."

"I love my niece." Mom grinned. "You're finally bringing a girl home. I can already tell I'll like Becky a lot more than I liked Miley."

"I like Becky a lot more than I like Miley. Most people would." Miley had a polarizing personality. He'd lost his rose-tinted glasses regarding Miley early last year.

"I hope to see more of Becky. Her accent is lovely."

"Don't get attached, Mom. She's going home in June."

"I don't think I'll be the one with an attachment problem. If you have feelings for her, you should consider exploring the possibility of a future together."

"Sorry, Mom. Not going to happen." He thought about kissing Becky too often. He blamed the fake relationship idea, and the whole town expecting him to be kissing her. Kissing Becky was a bad idea. Period.

"How's Dad doing?"

Mom frowned. "He's having a rough day."

"How rough?" He held back a sigh. Lately it seemed like Dad had more hard days than good days.

"He's not up to facing lunch. Since we have company, I'm not going to push him."

"Okay." Mom had more patience with Dad than he did. He prayed daily for Dad's health. There were supposed to be meds that could help. Sam didn't know if they made a difference, or if the side effects were worse than the benefits.

He moved his toolboxes to a corner of the deck, out of the way. He wouldn't be working on the Chevy this afternoon. Mom needed a nap, and he'd talk to the girls about what they wanted to do after lunch. They could detour into Wichita on the way home. In his limited experience, girls never said no to visiting a mall.

His parents' situation concerned him. Mom was under a lot of pressure. He understood Dad's health challenges weren't his fault. Dad didn't intend to make Mom's life difficult.

What could he do to make Mom's life easier? He'd had more time to visit during the week when they lived in Gilead. Until Easter, he'd be foot to the floor with work and the performance schedule. Dad refused to travel to Colorado more than once a year. It was hard for Mom. She missed her brother and family. The only thing Sam could do for his parents was to pray.

CHAPTER 9

$\mathcal{B}$ecky woke early on Monday morning and prepared for her daily walk into town and around campus. Her walk would include a clandestine meeting with Logan Miles. He'd sent her a text on Saturday, wanting to meet in person.

She'd slept well after enjoying a day out with Sam and Cindy. Sam's mom was lovely, and she'd made Becky feel welcome. They'd visited a mall in Wichita on the way home, a handy stop and an opportunity for Becky to buy neutral-toned sweats and hoodies. Logan's suggestion — wear clothes that were ordinary and wouldn't draw attention.

Becky missed the convenience of city living, and even the Wichita mall was tiny when compared to home. Last night, after Sam had dropped them back at the dorm, Cindy had shared her thoughts on her uncle and his long-term health issues. It was a hard situation. Becky had added Sam's parents to her prayer list.

Logan had planned to walk with her after she stopped by Heavenly Brew to collect her morning coffee. She'd let him know when she arrived at Heavenly Brew.

She pulled on her warm black hoodie and new black scarf. Her pale pink beanie would warm her head. She'd hide her hair and beanie in the hoodie when she left Heavenly Brew. The paparazzi hadn't tracked Logan to Gilead, but it was only a matter of time until his cover was blown.

Becky headed outdoors into the bitter February weather. She found the cold invigorating, and it reminded her of walking along the beach on a windy winter day. Back home, she'd walk by the ocean in all weather, including rain. Sometimes Dad would tag along. His hospital schedule made it hard to plan regular early morning walks. She valued that time with Dad where they could talk without interruption.

Since arriving in Gilead, she'd video call with Mum a few times a week, and Dad at least once a week. On Saturdays, Australian time, the whole family chatted on a video call. She missed seeing her family in person.

The aroma of coffee called her inside Heavenly Brew. The cowbell over the door clanged, and she shot a message to Logan. He'd told her to not look around and try to find him. Easier said than done.

Mrs. Alleghany stood at the bakery case, chatting with Letty. Letty noticed Becky and called her over. There was no line, and Mrs. Alleghany had Letty cornered behind the counter.

Letty smiled. "Morning, Becky. Your usual?"

"Yes, please."

Mrs. Alleghany took over the conversation. "Have you heard about poor Leo? He broke his arm riding a push-bike. Fancy that."

Hmm. She tapped her card and paid her for coffee. "Who told you that story?" A tall story with not even a shred of truth.

"I can't remember, dear. He's lost his chance to get discovered like our John Johnson. A terrible disappointment."

She nodded and pressed her lips together. If Mrs. Alleghany only knew the truth, which was a juicer story than she'd concocted. Leo had injured himself while doing a handstand on the back of a horse. The broken leg had put a crimp in Leo's dream to pursue stunt work for TV and movies.

Becky thanked Letty for her coffee and walked outside. She pulled on her hood and continued her usual route along Main Street. A guy in a gray hoodie crossed the street ahead of her. Logan. She kept walking and he was soon beside her, matching her pace.

"Hi, Bek. Thanks for agreeing to meet me."

"What's going on, Logan? Why are you here?"

"It's a long story. My life is different now to when you knew me in Australia."

"Okay." She sipped her coffee. The Logan she remembered was a hedonistic playboy with a white powder habit. She'd seen him high more often than sober.

"I hit rock-bottom last year. After I returned to the States. I was drinking too much. Taking too many drugs."

It was good he'd recognized he'd had a problem. "Did you go to rehab?"

"Yeah. My mentor, John Johnson, took me under his wing. Helped me clean up. Led me to Jesus."

"You're a Christian." Wow. She had wondered, since the passion play was very Christian. *Thank you, Jesus.* He'd saved Logan from a path that led to destruction.

"My faith journey hasn't been easy. I've made a lot of mistakes. Hurt a lot of people."

"Haven't we all." She'd made her share of mistakes.

"I'd like to talk more, but the paps will be sniffing around soon. I don't want you dragged into the spotlight. I'm assuming you're calling yourself Becky because you're hiding in Gilead."

"That's right. After everything blew up with Jarrod, I had to get away."

"Did he treat you badly?"

"He cheated on me." Her gut tightened. "The photos were splashed over the internet for the world to see."

"I'm sorry, Bek. He's not a good guy."

"I know that now." Jarrod had said he was happy to wait for intimacy until they'd married. He'd attended church with her. He'd said and done all the right Christian things in public. He'd talked about whisking her away to Bali and proposing on a tropical beach at sunset. The paparazzi had exposed his double life and sent her running to the other side of the world.

"Bek, I'd like to chat more. As friends. I promise I'm not hitting on you."

She nodded. "I'd like to hear your story. Hear more about how you met Jesus."

"For sure. The paps will make it tricky. I want to protect your privacy."

"I understand and appreciate that." Jarrod's thirst for media attention had destroyed her privacy. "The town will soon be full of visitors. That could make it easier to blend in."

"Or it could make it harder to spot the paps and their cameras. I have limited options for where I live and how I can give them the slip. I've got a couple of guys on standby to work as my lookalikes and confuse everyone."

"A good idea."

"That's why I don't want you looking for me. You'll see my doubles around town. Approaching them in front of the paps will expose you to unnecessary scrutiny."

"Sure." She walked along a tree-lined path on campus. It was beautiful and quiet, but there were plenty of places to hide in bushes or climb trees. "What about the play? I can't avoid you there."

"Your boyfriend will take care of you." Logan's voice softened. "I can tell he's protective and everyone speaks highly of Sam."

"Okay." She loved that Sam would protect her. She'd only seen Logan at one rehearsal, and he'd already pegged her and Sam as a couple.

"I'll leave you to finish your walk. I trust you to keep my secret. I'll keep yours as well."

"Thanks, Logan."

"Take care, Bek." He chose a different route at the fork in the path, leading him back toward town.

She lengthened her stride, her mind swirling. Logan was a Christian. That news would keep her smiling all day. When would he publicly share his faith? She hadn't followed his career since he left Australia.

He'd taken a risk in meeting her. She'd follow his lead and protect his privacy. Who would have thought she'd move to Kansas and become friends with Logan Miles?

She'd contacted her sister, Mel, and line up a video call. She needed to talk to someone about Logan. Someone who wasn't in Gilead. Mel was the one person she trusted to keep Logan's secret.

SAM STOOD BACKSTAGE, arms crossed over his chest, assessing the props and mentally ticking off his to-do list. It was opening night, and the play would commence soon. He'd arrived early with Cindy and Becky, then gone on ahead into the auditorium while the girls made a detour via the petting zoo. Why they'd want to see donkeys was beyond him. Horses, he could under-stand. Donkeys? No.

Becky appeared by his side, bouncing on her toes as if she'd drunk two gallons of coffee. "The donkeys are adorable. You're right about the kiddos loving the petting zoo."

He rolled his eyes. "They're not adorable if you've got to clean up their mess."

"Eww. I didn't consider bodily functions. Someone would have that job, right?"

"Glad it's not me." He clapped his hands together. "We're ready to roll. So far nothing has gone wrong."

Her smile lit up her eyes. "That's a relief. I'm so excited to see the play tonight."

"I'll spend most of my time with you beside the stage. Take the opportunity to enjoy the full play experience."

"I will. I can't wait."

Becky practically skipped ahead to their position near the stage.

He followed, his mind focused on his small role in this larger performance. And he prayed. God knew who'd be sitting in those auditorium seats, watching the action unfold on the stage. He prayed their hearts would be touched by the hand of Jesus as they walked with Him on His journey to the cross and His resurrection.

Becky was enthralled by the opening night performance. A myriad of emotions, and tears, were visible on her face.

His phone vibrated in his pocket mid-act. Had something gone wrong backstage? He checked the screen. It was Cindy.

Becky pulled her phone out of her pocket. Had Cindy messaged her, too?

He read the message. Six words. Logan Miles is in the house.

What? Why was that important? His name sounded kind of familiar. Cindy seemed to think Sam would know this Logan.

Sam glanced at Becky. She stared at her phone screen, her face pale. An unusual reaction. Had she received the same message from Cindy?

He tucked his phone back in his pocket. Becky typed something into her phone. He shuffled over and stood behind her shoulder. She moved her phone screen out of view. Interesting. Did she have something to hide?

The act ended. They did their set moving routine and returned to their positions.

"Becky." He placed his hand on her shoulder. "Is everything okay?

"Yeah, I'm good."

"Did Cindy message you about Logan Miles?"

She nodded. "You know who he is, right?"

"Why would I know him?"

"He's a famous Hollywood actor." She narrowed her eyes. "Do you watch action movies?"

He shrugged. "Sometimes. Where is this Logan guy?"

"Cindy didn't say. You can ask her at the after-party."

"I will." The next act started and they watched it together in silence. The after-party would be held in the college cafeteria. He often skipped the parties, but the girls were keen to attend. Cindy had volunteered to help organize the party. Becky had suggested their attendance together would be expected. She wasn't wrong. The crew talked about Becky being his girl. If only that was true…

The applause died down, and the actors made their final exit from the stage. Sam and Becky sprung into action, resetting the stage for the first act in the next performance. They'd save time not having to pack up everything after each performance, and then having to do the reset before the next performance.

They finished packing up and left the backstage area.

Sam spotted Cindy in the foyer.

"Becky." Cindy rushed over, eyes wide and voice loud. "Can you believe it? Logan Miles is here. In Gilead."

"Hang on." He turned to his cousin. "Back up a bit. Who is Logan Miles? Why should I care?"

"Oh, Sam. Do you live under a rock? He's a famous actor and he's performing in our play."

"What do you mean by performing?" He'd missed something important. He couldn't recall anyone named Logan being on the cast list. If Logan was here, why hadn't anyone recognized him?

"He's the new Judas."

"What? His name's Miles."

"Yes. Logan Miles. He's seriously rich and seriously famous and he's here. In Gilead."

"Calm down. You'll scare him out of town if you keep on like this."

Becky hadn't joined in with Cindy's fangirl hysterics. His opinion of Becky rose another notch.

"How did you find out he's here?" he asked.

"During the play. The teen girls who were sitting beside me are massive Logan Miles fans. We had great seats. Very close to the stage. The girls thought they recognized the guy playing Judas. He was obviously talented, but no one knew anything about him. His name didn't show up in online searches. Then something clicked after intermission. They joined the dots and uploaded photos. Others in the audience uploaded photos and started chatting. Everyone got excited. It's a whole thing."

Becky frowned. "People were on their phones during the play? Isn't that rude?"

"Teen girls live online." Cindy shrugged. "They rushed out to the lobby during the play to stalk the backstage exits."

He shook his head. "They harassed a man because he looked like a famous actor."

"But they knew they were right." Cindy placed her hands on her hips. "Someone on crew tipped them off that Miles had left early. The girls returned to their seats and told me the whole story when the play ended."

"Miles might have felt sick or something." Cindy yelling like a fifteen-year-old at a rock concert would bring on a headache. "He's a recluse. Keeps to himself."

"Exactly." Cindy nodded. "Logan is hiding here, and his cover is blown. Someone tipped him off and he disappeared."

"I'm hungry. And thirsty." Becky caught Cindy's attention. "Can we head over to the party?"

"Shoot." Cindy glanced at her phone. "I'm supposed to be there now. Catch you later."

Cindy took off, weaving through the crowd who lingered near the auditorium entrance.

He turned to Becky. "I don't understand the whole celebrity thing. My cousin has lost her mind."

"Yeah. It's crazy. If what Cindy's saying is true, we'll see more security and photographers in town."

"Good point. There's more security when John Johnson makes an appearance."

"Is he in town?"

"No idea." He paused. "Please don't tell me you want to stalk John Johnson."

She chuckled. "I don't want to stalk anyone. Who would want to be a celebrity?"

"Not me." An insane amount of attention from screaming teen girls was the stuff of nightmares. Was Miles really a famous actor in disguise? Cindy's story sounded like one of Mrs. Alleghany's exaggerated stories.

Becky smiled. "We need to make an appearance at the party."

"Yeah. Let's go." He walked with Becky toward the cafeteria. She seemed lost in her own thoughts.

Hopefully whatever had bothered Becky earlier was sorted. If what Cindy had shared was true, then everyone would be talking about Miles being Logan Miles. Which meant they'd all forget about him and Becky. A blessing in disguise.

Sam was drawn to Becky and struggling to hide his growing feelings. That was scary. He shouldn't be contemplating the idea of a future with Becky. It wasn't possible. It couldn't happen. She might not reciprocate his feelings, and it was pointless to chase a dream and risk rejection. Besides, Becky wouldn't fit into his Colorado ranch plans.

❀

THE FOLLOWING AFTERNOON, Becky made a pot of hot green tea and curled up on the recliner in her dorm room. Her classes were finished for the day, and her assignments were on track. She had time to rest and relax before she made dinner. The frozen meals stockpiled in her freezer from the ranch were a time-saving blessing.

She poured a cup of tea and checked the time on her phone. Mel should be calling any minute. Her sister had set her alarm for six in the morning to squeeze in a video call. Becky would be busy with the play tomorrow and Saturday, making it harder to coordinate calls with her family.

Her phone buzzed and Becky connected the video call. "Hey, Mel. It's good to see you."

"You too, lil sis."

The childhood nickname choked up her throat. Tears threatened. She missed her family, but she wasn't going to cry. She'd had severe homesickness last year. She was stronger now and had done therapy to build resilience.

She sucked in a deep breath. "Sorry to wake you early. Have you had coffee?"

"Mum's making it now. Dad's here, too."

"Excellent. I'll say hello before we chat."

Her parents' precious faces filled her phone screen. They asked her a bunch of mundane questions, and she reassured them that she was okay. Life in Gilead was good. God would help her manage her present circumstances.

Being the youngest child had drawbacks. Mum had trouble letting go. The time apart would improve their relationship.

Her parents left the room, and she gained Mel's undivided attention.

"What I'm about to share is confidential."

"Bek, are you in trouble?"

"No. I'm fine."

"Thank goodness. I was worried you'd got caught up in a bad relationship or something."

That concern was valid. Mel had seen Jarrod's true character and tried to warn her. It wasn't Mel's fault that she hadn't listened and messed up everything.

"This situation is connected to Jarrod."

"How? Does Jarrod know you're in Gilead?"

She shook her head. The last thing she wanted was for Jarrod to find her in Gilead. "Remember how Jarrod was friends with Logan Miles?"

Mel nodded. "You stayed at Logan's beach house in Byron Bay."

"A memory I'd rather forget." Jarrod and Logan hadn't hidden their love for the white powder. She'd declined their offer to partake, appalled that she'd missed seeing signs of Jarrod's drug use. She was naïve. He was an actor who'd hidden his vices.

Jarrod and Logan had partied together in LA a few years earlier. Jarrod had failed to make it in Hollywood and had returned to Australia with a chip on his shoulder the size of Texas. Then he'd landed a supporting role in Logan's action movie that was filmed in Australia.

"Have you heard from Logan?" Mel asked. "He disappeared off the celebrity radar. Kelly mentioned it the other day."

"Interesting." Kelly had introduced her to Jarrod. Becky prayed her sister would quit the party scene, return to church and follow Mel's example. "Logan is hiding out in Gilead."

"He's what? No. Why's he in Kansas?"

"You won't believe this. Logan has a role in the passion play. He's Leo's replacement for Judas."

Mel's eyes widened. "And no one has recognized him. How?"

"That's the problem. A group of girls recognized him last night. Thankfully, Cindy was sitting next to them and sent me a text. I sent Logan a text to warn him. He left early, right after the act where Judas kills himself, and escaped seeing the girls."

"Hang on. Why are you texting Logan? Aren't you dating Sam?"

"Logan gave me his number. We're friends. Nothing more. And guess what he told me? He's done rehab and become a Christian."

"Wow. That's amazing."

"It is. I'm seeing Logan tomorrow."

"How are you keeping the meetings secret? Are the paps in town?"

"Not yet. Logan meets me during my walks. We walk and talk. Wear hoodies and sunglasses."

"It sounds like you're in a spy movie."

She laughed. "It's weird. Cindy's a big Logan fan, but I can't let on that I know him."

"That's awkward. Does Sam know? What's happening with Sam?"

"Logan has sworn me to secrecy. Sam doesn't know anything. Everyone thinks I'm dating Sam. Including Logan."

"But you're fake dating Sam, right?"

She closed her eyes. She wouldn't lie to her sister. "Yes and no."

"What do you mean?"

"I like dating Sam, and it doesn't feel fake anymore. We're friends. Good friends. I'm getting attached."

"Whoa. You have feelings for Sam. When did that happen?"

"I was attracted to Sam from the start. But it doesn't have to mean anything. I ignored the attraction and we friend zoned each other. Everything was fine."

"What changed?"

"Our friendship. It's getting stronger and deeper, and I love so many things about him. His faith is solid, Mel. Rock solid. He's a great guy."

Mel grinned. "You're falling for him."

She let out a long sigh. "It can't work. He's a cowboy. I'm

leaving."

"Pray about Sam. Seek God's wisdom and guidance."

"I will." Could she have a future with Sam?

"Back to Logan. What's going on with him?"

"He expects the paps to turn up anytime. He's trying to protect my privacy." Unlike Jarrod.

"You've been photographed with Logan. That could be a problem."

"I know." Too many photos of her with Jarrod and Logan in Sydney and Byron Bay. Photos that included Logan's casual flings, the girls who'd used Logan to further their modeling and influencer ambitions.

Her January vacation in Byron Bay last year was the beginning of the end of her relationship with Jarrod. His lies had started to unravel, and his double life had been exposed by the paps he'd tried to woo to improve his acting career and celebrity status.

"What are you going to do, Bek? If you're photographed with Logan, the world will know you're in Gilead."

"I'll be careful. Please pray. I want to support Logan. He's a baby Christian who needs Christian friends. John Johnson's the mentor who introduced him to Jesus."

"That's a cool story. I hope Logan shares it with the world soon."

"Me too. But it's Logan's story to tell when he's ready. I have to keep his secret. I can't tell Cindy. I can't even tell Sam."

"That's rough. Hiding stuff from Sam isn't a good idea."

"I don't have a choice. I promised Logan."

"I'll be praying."

"Thanks. I need your prayers." Mel would let her know if she heard anything about Logan Miles. Becky loved both of her sisters, but she couldn't trust Kelly with this secret. There was no need to involve Mum and Dad. Or Zach and Billie. She prayed Logan would continue to find peace in Gilead.

CHAPTER 10

The next day, Becky finished her last Friday afternoon class and dashed back to her dorm. She changed into sweats and pulled a gray hoodie over her head. Logan had lined up a meeting near the petting zoo to talk about the fact he'd been recognized.

She grabbed a new pair of sunglasses and headed out before her dorm friends had a chance to sidetrack her. The petting zoo was an ideal place to meet. Tourists gathered there. The adults would be watching their kids and the animals rather than the people around them.

A second walk today was good for her health. Better than the gym. She took the long route with fewer people on the path and mingled with the small crowd at the petting zoo. A group of cute kids surrounded the donkeys. Parents had their phones out, snapping photos. She stayed on the edge of the crowd, stepping back to allow newcomers to take a closer look.

Logan appeared beside her. She ignored him, waiting for him to break the silence.

He pointed at the donkeys. "Here's the plan. I'll hold your

hand and we'll act like a couple. Follow my lead, and we'll go to the pond on campus."

"Okay." Logan had done his homework. There was a bench seat shaded by a tree where they could talk without being overheard.

Logan touched her fingertips and settled his hand over hers. She felt nothing. No tingles. No hint of attraction. It was like holding her father's hand or brother's hand. A polar opposite experience to holding Sam's hand.

Her stomach lurched. What would Sam think if he caught her holding hands with Logan? Her life was upside down crazy.

Logan tugged her hand and she followed, falling into step beside him.

"Are you okay with the hand holding?" he asked.

"Yeah. As long as you're not hitting on me." It had to be said. Boundaries were important.

He chuckled. "You're the first female to say that to me in a long time."

"Get used to it, buddy. I speak my mind." Therapy had helped build her self-confidence.

"Good for you." He loosened his grip on her hand. "Sam's a lucky guy. I'm not in the right headspace to think about romantic relationships."

"That's fair." She smiled and nodded at the people they passed. She didn't recognize anyone. Thankfully. More importantly, no one stopped or looked like they'd recognized her.

Before long they reached a vacant bench seat. She leaned against the backrest and turned to Logan. "Any sign of the paps?"

"Not yet. But the word is out and they'll be around. There aren't many tickets available for the performances."

"That's good news." A full house of people who'd hear about Jesus.

He nodded. "My doubles are in town. If we meet again on a

performance day, the petting zoo will work. We'll do the hand-holding thing so you'll know it's me."

"Sure. What about the play?"

"We'll be professional. Sam expects me to stop and chat. If you're around, just treat me like any other actor."

"Okay." Logan wasn't like any other actor. She'd try to play it cool. "What about the cast and crew?"

"I'm praying they'll be supportive and understand my desire for privacy."

"I hope they will." Cindy would have had trouble keeping her fangirling under control if she was volunteering this year.

"They've seen how intrusive the paps have been in John's life. John thinks it will be fine."

"Good point." John Johnson was the favorite town celebrity. "The Gilead folk look out for each other."

He nodded. "I'd love to talk more about the Bible and verses I'm reading. I don't know many Christians. I can't expect to attend a church service and not get recognized."

"That would be tricky." She was a nobody, yet still felt like people watched her and Sam at church. Logan had star power that drew attention from across the country.

"Yeah." He adjusted his baseball cap. "I'm not ready to go public with my faith journey."

"I understand and I'll be praying for you." It was a privilege to have an opportunity to talk with Logan about her faith. Could they meet and avoid the cameras? She prayed for wisdom. She prayed Sam would understand if he found out about her secret meetings with Logan.

Her not-so-fake relationship with Sam was complicated. The time would come when she'd need to make a decision. Was she willing to start a real relationship with Sam and trust God to guide her in His will?

～

A WEEK LATER, Becky sat beside Cindy at a cafeteria table — or the dining hall, as Cindy and the other students called it. The line had grown and the tables would soon fill with people.

An early dinner worked with Becky's schedule. She didn't need to rush her meal and she'd have time for dessert. She picked at her half-eaten plate of beef stroganoff. The serving sizes were generous, and she wanted to leave room for apple crumble.

She sipped her water. "How's the essay going?"

"Nearly done." Cindy ate another mouthful of the delicious beef. "I'll work on it tonight."

"Good plan." Becky glanced around the spacious dining area. She waved at students she recognized from her classes. People watching was fun.

Cindy paused, her fork mid-air. "I don't believe it."

"Believe what?" She followed Cindy's gaze, focused on the line in the serving area.

"We have a billionaire in the house."

"Huh." She wrinkled her brows. "That doesn't seem likely." Gilead wasn't billionaire central.

"It's him. For sure."

"Who?"

"The guy standing beside Wendy. You know her. She's the lady in the office who always looks sad."

"Yeah. The quiet one." Last year, Dad had asked her to speak with Wendy about making a donation to the college. Wendy had provided a few options and Dad had wired the money.

"He's the billionaire from Chicago who everyone's talking about."

"Not everyone." A billionaire on campus was news to her. Logan Miles was bigger news.

"Why would a billionaire eat dinner in our humble dining hall?"

She smiled and pointed to her plate. "Because the beef stroganoff is good. That's why I'm here."

"But he could eat anywhere. Fly in food from Chicago in his private jet."

"Seriously? That sounds insane."

"It happens. I saw it on a reality TV show."

Becky rolled her eyes. "Stop watching trash. Billionaires are just people like us who happen to have a lot of money."

"I've never met a billionaire." Cindy sighed. "Logan Miles is rich and famous, but even he's not a billionaire."

"Billionaires and celebrities can be normal people." Her parents' lifelong friends who owned the horse stud were billionaires. They'd made bank on energy sector investments, and the family fortune had skyrocketed into Australia's rich list.

Cindy shook her head. "I'm not convinced. Money changes people. Sometimes ruins them."

"I won't argue that point. The love of money gets a lot of people into trouble."

"Exactly." Cindy grasped Becky's forearm. "Don't look up. Corey is alone, carrying his tray and heading in our direction."

"Oh boy. I'll ignore him." She stared at her plate and focused on eating. He could be meeting friends at a nearby table. He might want to eat alone and listen to a podcast. He'd recommended a couple of history podcasts during class the other day. She'd tune in and listen after Easter when she regained leisure time.

"Hi, Becky. Cindy. Can I join you for dinner?" Corey asked.

She looked up. He wore the hopeful puppy dog expression that felt mean to reject.

"Sure." It wasn't like she had a choice. It was only dinner. Cindy was here.

His face brightened and he sat opposite. "How's the play going?"

"Good." She moved food around on her plate. "I'm busy juggling the play and my studies." The same old line she trotted out every time Corey showed an interest in her life… which was at least once a week.

"Too busy for church. I see Cindy on Sundays, but you're never there."

"No." Cindy jumped in, her tone defensive. "We've already told you Becky is going to church with my cousin."

He turned to Becky. "That's now a permanent thing."

"Until I go home in June." Becky reined in her frustration at covering the same ground with Corey over and over. She wasn't interested in dating Corey. Why couldn't he acknowledge and accept it?

"Don't mind me. I'll pray the blessing before I eat." Corey closed his eyes, his lips moving as if he was talking aloud.

She exchanged a glance with Cindy. Corey wouldn't take their gentle hints. He asked Cindy about her every Sunday morning after church. He sat near her in class and tried to engage her in conversation. It had progressed past awkward and shifted toward creepy territory. She prayed Corey would open his ears and listen.

Corey opened his eyes and smiled. "Becky, did you receive your essay results?"

She nodded. "I haven't had a chance to read the comments." She was pleased with her mark on the King David essay. A fair result for the time and effort she'd invested.

"My essay mark topped the class."

"Congratulations." Becky wasn't surprised. He'd told her he'd spent hours researching Solomon. More hours than she'd spent on researching and writing her own essay.

"Would you like to read it?" he asked.

She chewed on the beef and their conversation topic. Her thoughts on Solomon and his lust problem hadn't changed. There were parallels between Solomon and Logan. Both men were rich and influential. Logan had women throwing themselves at him, but that didn't mean he had to engage and indulge their desire for intimacy. He'd chosen celibacy during his recovery. He acknowledged that women were a temptation that could derail his sobriety.

Becky swallowed her mouthful of stroganoff. Slowly. Buying time. "I'm too busy with the play."

"Okay. What about you, Cindy?"

Cindy shook her head. "I'm good. I've already passed that subject."

He turned to Becky. "After Easter, we could talk about our essays."

"Probably not." Definitely not. When would he listen? "My schedule is pretty full."

Cindy folded her arms across her torso. "Becky is dating my cousin. They spend a lot of time together, and that will likely continue after Easter."

Corey drank his iced tea, his cheeks ballooning.

Becky widened her eyes. She'd be cranky if he sprayed a mouthful of soda across the table.

He swallowed, his face flushed. "Are you serious about this guy?"

She nodded. "Sam is the only guy I'm interested in dating." It was the truth.

"Will you change your mind?" he asked.

"No. I don't know if we can be friends if you have a problem with Sam."

Corey's flushed face deepened into fire engine red territory. "I like you, Becky. A lot. But I accept we can only be friends."

"Thank you." This conversation with Corey was hard work. She prayed Corey would direct his romantic interest elsewhere. Find someone suitable for him.

Sam was the man who'd captured Becky's interest. The man she thought about kissing, until she remembered why that was a bad idea. But she could dream about a happily-ever-after with Sam, even if it was unlikely to happen in real life.

THE FOLLOWING WEEK, Sam pressed end on a phone call from the hospital ER where Mom worked. She'd complained of a headache and collapsed during her shift. Her blood pressure had spiked, and they were running tests. Please, Lord, help the doctors work out what's going on with Mom's health.

Fridays were usually his shortest workday. He'd started work at a ranch near Gilead early this morning, knowing he had enough maintenance work to keep him busy until mid-afternoon. He'd call his boss and reschedule the routine work at Walker Ridge Ranch. Mom needed him.

He headed for the stables and spotted a familiar face. Noah had scored the role of Loginus, a centurion in the play. Sam explained his family situation to Noah and returned to his truck. He repacked his tools, double-checking he hadn't forgotten anything. He was thankful he'd packed a boxed lunch this morning and could make the ninety-minute drive to the hospital without a food detour.

He switched on the engine and called Dad. No answer. The hospital had said they'd tried Dad first, since he was Mom's first emergency contact, and couldn't get through to him. Dad was on a new med that he'd claimed made him sleepy in the mornings. Maybe he'd slept through the phone calls.

Sam turned onto the highway and drove back toward Gilead. Of course, the ranch was on the side of town that was furthest away from Mom. The minutes ticked by and he hit traffic as he navigated his way through the busy town center to the hospital parking lot. At least he found a parking space that accommodated his truck.

He collected his lunch from the passenger seat and walked to the ER entrance. The lady at the reception desk directed him to an exam room. It was empty, the bed missing. A nurse let him know Mom was having scans done.

Sam made himself comfortable in a plastic chair and started on lunch. Better to eat now, in case Mom was feeling nauseous.

He sent Cindy a short text. Within seconds she called him.

"Sam, what's happening?"

"Mom's having tests. Can you let your parents know?"

"Of course. Mom will probably drive over and stay with your folks. Is your dad with you?"

"No. He's not answering the phone."

"I hope he's okay."

"Yeah. He says his new meds make him sleepy. That could be the reason."

"I'm sorry. Is there anything I can do?" Cindy sounded concerned.

"If you see Becky, please tell her to contact me. I'll send her a text when I know what's happening. We're supposed to be meeting for an early dinner, but I don't know if I'll be back in time."

"Where's dinner?"

"On campus at the dining hall."

"If a guy called Corey stops by to talk to Becky in the dining hall, make sure you look like a couple."

"Why? Who's this Corey guy?"

"Becky hasn't mentioned him?"

"Not a word. Should I know about him?" Now he was curious. Was Becky interested in dating Corey?

"He's a student who attends my church. He likes Becky but she's not interested."

"Is he being inappropriate?"

"Not at the moment. I was there when she told him she's not interested, but I'm not convinced he's listening."

His hand formed a fist. That wouldn't fix the situation. "What can I do?"

"If you ever meet Corey, then act like you're in love with Becky."

He nodded. He was no actor, but he didn't need to try and pretend he had feelings for Becky. The feelings were there, and he was in a quandary.

The door opened and Mom's bed was wheeled into the room.

"Mom's back. I have to go."

"Sure. Keep me posted."

"Will do." He stood and reached for Mom's hand. "How are you doing?"

"Tired. Glad you're here, but I feel bad. You're missing work."

"It's okay. You're more important than work."

"I love you, Sam." Mom looked around. "Where's your father?"

"I don't know. He didn't answer the phone."

Mom let out a sob and closed her eyes. Tears dripped from between her lashes, landing on her pale face.

He squeezed her hand. "Mom, what's going on with Dad?"

"I can't keep doing this."

"Doing what?"

She opened her watery eyes and held his gaze. "Carrying your father. Working all the time. It's too much."

He nodded. "I thought you were planning to retire soon."

"That's the problem. I can't."

"Sure you can quit your job and retire."

Mom blew out a long breath. "I can, but we'd need to move. It's too expensive to stay here."

He did the math and it wasn't adding up. "You'll have your retirement benefits, right?"

"Not yet. I can't access those funds until I'm older."

"You have your share in the ranch. Maybe I could buy —"

"No. I don't have any shares left."

"What do you mean? I don't follow." Uncle Joe had said she'd sold back some of her share of the ranch. Not her whole share. But he'd backpedaled when Sam had asked for specific details. It was Mom's business to tell Sam, not his uncle's.

"Over the years, when we've been short of funds, I sold most of my share back to Joe."

"Why didn't you tell me?" He could have helped. Perhaps not when he was in high school or college, but in the last few years.

"My father set up the inheritance trust for you. The trust remains intact and you have your family legacy. Since your father will only visit the ranch for a few days over Christmas…"

Dad was the reason. He'd pushed Mom to sell. It explained a lot. His father and uncle didn't get along. Now he knew why Uncle Joe was careful in what he'd said regarding Mom and her share in the ranch. There was no money at the ranch to help Mom retire.

"So what's your plan?" She had a plan, right? Mom always had a plan.

"I'll still retire to the ranch. I've spoken at length with Joe and Lori. Even if you don't settle at the ranch, I can pay my way and make it work."

"What do you mean, I? What about Dad?"

"Your father is stubborn. I didn't want to leave Gilead, but he insisted his health would improve if we moved here closer to his family."

He nodded. Dad's health was about the same. Possibly worse than before the move. "Has his health improved?"

Mom shook her head. "I miss you. I miss my family being nearby. I miss Colorado."

He could relate. "What does Dad want?"

"To stay here. But I'm stressed and miserable. My friends from church are in Gilead, and I'm too busy working to see them. Too busy working to make new friends here. Your father hardly leaves the house."

Dad wasn't supporting Mom. His health issues were wrecking Mom's health.

He rubbed his hand over his face. This situation was worse than he'd imagined. "Is your blood pressure high due to stress?"

"Probably. It's been high for a while now. I'm on meds for that. And for migraines."

"What has your doctor suggested?"

"Exercise. Lose weight. Sleep more. Work less. Reduce stress."

He nodded. "That makes sense."

"I don't have time to exercise. Your father expects me to work and do everything at home. I don't get enough sleep. My migraine issues are getting worse. My boss is supportive and trying to help me out, but the problems at home are too big."

His blood pressure ramped up a notch. "Dad is a problem."

More tears escaped from between Mom's lashes. She used her sleeve to wipe them away. "I have vacation time accrued. Joe and Lori have invited me to stay at the ranch. I'm thinking about accepting their offer."

"Will Dad go to Colorado?"

She shook her head. "He point-blank refuses. He doesn't want me to go."

Stubborn old coot. Just because Dad's darkest days were connected to his recovery from the accident at the ranch didn't mean Mom should miss out. "Will Dad cope on his own?"

"I don't know." She shrugged. "All I know is I'm no good to anyone if I'm pushing up daisies."

His stomach sank faster than a torpedo fired at the ocean floor. No. He didn't want to think about Mom's mortality. Or Dad's unintended role in running her health into the ground. He was stuck in the middle. Their marriage was complicated. Relationships were complicated. His feelings for Becky were complicated.

He stood. "I'm going to visit Dad. Check he's okay."

"A good idea."

"I'll be back to check on you before I leave town. I'm supposed to be having an early dinner with Becky before the play."

"Oh, don't let me stop you from seeing Becky. She's a lovely girl."

He nodded and dropped a kiss on Mom's cheek. "I'll be back soon."

He left Mom and walked outside. He scanned the parking lot, searching for his truck. In his rush he'd forgotten to pay attention to where he'd parked. What a day.

He located his truck and drove to his parents' home. He had a front door key, in case Dad didn't answer.

He parked on the drive and walked over to the front door. He pressed the doorbell. No answer. He pressed it again. Still no answer.

He unlocked the door and walked inside. No sign of Dad in the living room. The kitchen was a mess. He opened a blind, letting in sunlight. He put the lid on the peanut butter and returned it to the pantry. Rinsed the plates, mugs, and flatware, and stacked the dishwasher the way Mom liked it. He found cleaning spray and paper towels, and wiped the kitchen counter. Cleaned up the spilled coffee granules and sugar.

He made his way to his parents' bedroom. The house was dark. All the curtains were drawn. He knocked on the door. "Dad, it's me."

The door cracked open a few inches. "I don't want to talk to you."

What? "Dad, what's going on?"

"It's your fault," Dad yelled.

"What's my fault?" He was missing something. Dad was aggressive, which wasn't normal. Was this a side effect from the new meds?

"Your mother leaving me to live at the ranch. It's your fault. If you weren't moving to Colorado, she'd be happy to stay. Go away. Leave me alone."

The bedroom door slammed in his face.

He felt like Dad had punched him hard in the solar plexus. Was it safe for Mom to be at home with Dad? He couldn't believe he was even asking the question.

Sam drove his truck around the corner and parked in a quiet street. He called Uncle Joe.

His uncle answered on the third ring. "Sam, what's happening?"

"Is Aunt Lori on her way here?"

"She's less than an hour from the hospital."

"I'm so glad to hear it."

"What's wrong, Sam?"

"Dad's in a bad way. I don't know if it's safe for Mom to go home."

Uncle Joe grunted. "We'll make a hotel reservation that includes your mother. Do you think your father might need to go to the hospital?"

"I'm not sure. A doctor would need to make that call." And Sam could just imagine Dad's reaction to a house call from his doctor.

"Where are you now?"

"I'm still in town. Close to the hospital."

"Okay. Meet Lori there and we'll put a plan together. You're needed back in Gilead for the play tonight, right?"

"Yeah, but I can stay —"

"No. Let us handle the situation with your parents. Pray for your mom. Pray we can get your dad the help he needs."

"Thank you." He appreciated Uncle Joe's support. They'd helped Mom other times when Dad's mental health wasn't great. They knew the drill.

Sam would drive back to the hospital and wait for Aunt Lori. He should have enough time to return to Gilead for dinner with Becky.

How could he become Switzerland? Neutral and supportive, and not taking sides. He prayed for his parents. For their health. For their marriage. For his sanity as he navigated the rough waters in his family.

CHAPTER 11

$\mathcal{A}$ week later, Sam drove Becky to his home after church to swap vehicles. They'd stopped by Heavenly Brew and bought lunch to take on their road trip. Becky wanted to see hills, they didn't have a lot of time, and his Cadillac Eldorado needed a good run.

He pulled into his drive and parked his truck to the side, leaving space for the Cadillac to pass.

Becky unclipped her seat belt, her gaze on his home.

"Nice place, Sam."

"It's small, only two bedrooms. I'm tidying the yard and fixing stuff. Hope to sell it by summer."

Her eyes widened. "That's exciting. A big move."

"It is and it isn't. My folks moved away and there's no family here, other than Cindy. I'm ready for a new challenge at the ranch."

"I'm happy for you." She hopped out of his truck and wandered around his front garden. The tulip bulbs were in full bloom, adding color to the flower beds.

He headed around the back and opened the old garage door. His large shed was his mechanical work area, with his Cadillac filling a lot of the space. Cherry red. Gleaming chrome. Restored with help from Dad prior to his parents leaving Gilead.

His '68 Chevy needed work. The project he'd been working on for years with Dad's help. Dad's reluctance to visit Gilead had slowed their progress to a snail's pace.

He filled the trunk with essential tools, water, and oil. Checked the spare tire was inflated. If they broke down, he could repair and fix most minor mechanical problems with his tools.

If only he had the tools to fix his broken parents. Mom's scans had come back clear and her physical health had stabilized. Aunt Lori had taken Mom to the ranch after Mom was discharged from hospital. Mom was using her vacation time and planned to stay at the ranch until Easter.

Dad was at home and refusing treatment at the hospital. He'd visited his doctor, who'd adjusted Dad's meds and confirmed Dad's physical health was okay.

Sam had spoken with the mental health team who were assisting Dad by making home visits. Mom's health emergency, and her decision to rest at the ranch, was Dad's wake-up call. He'd apologized to Sam. Dad's anger had spurred him into action, and Sam was hopeful. He prayed his parents could nego-tiate a win-win solution to save their marriage.

Becky walked into the shed. "You've got a great setup. My dad would love it."

"He restores old cars."

"Not as often as he'd like. He's too busy with work."

Sam nodded and tossed his house keys in her direction.

She caught them in one hand.

"Good catch."

She grinned. "I was good at cricket."

"Cricket. What's that?"

"A kind of ball game. One of Dad's favorites. I think you'd like it."

"Okay then." He'd look up cricket online later. "Water bottles are in the fridge. Bathroom is off the hall."

"Thanks. I'm assuming we're not driving to a mall in Wichita."

He shook his head. "Opposite direction with limited rest stops."

"Sounds fun." She left the shed.

He'd tidied his home earlier this morning, ensuring it was clean. He wasn't cleaning his parents' home. That was Dad's responsibility, and it would give Dad something constructive to do that would occupy his time and help Mom.

Sam ducked indoors and found his cooler bag for the drinks. He locked up the house, stowed their supplies in the back of the Cadillac behind the front seat, and slid into the driver's side bench seat.

Becky opened the passenger door and placed her purse between them. "A fifties model."

"You're close. Sixties."

He reversed his car out of the shed, closed the garage door, and returned to the car. He maneuvered the Cadillac onto his street and gave her the rundown on the car specs as he took the road heading south out of town.

Sam was impressed Becky knew what he was talking about and shared his interest in cars. She never failed to surprise him. They had more in common than he'd guessed when they'd first met on the blind date.

"Are we keeping the top on the car?" she asked.

He nodded. "It's too windy and dusty. Plus sunburn."

"Good point. Can I guess where we're going?"

"Sure." This could be fun.

"We're on the highway traveling south, and I can't see any hills. Oklahoma."

"Well done. Have you visited?"

"No, and I didn't know there were hills in Oklahoma. I thought it was flat, like Kansas."

"These are special type of hills. If you're thinking rolling green hills like England, you're on the wrong track."

"Oh." She clasped her hands together. "This is exciting, and the car is purring."

"The way I like it." He'd filled the gas tank and given the Cadillac a full service. The engine additives made a difference and helped with performance.

"Can I cheat and open the maps app on my phone?" she asked.

"No. A map won't help."

"How come?"

"The place we're going has two names. Neither are an accurate description, according to my Colorado standards."

"The Rockies are magnificent."

"The best." The ranch was a long drive from Denver and the Rockies. He'd love to have time to explore the mountains and visit the small towns. He'd caught Becky's travel bug.

"I'll be patient and stare at the cornfields."

He chuckled and changed gears using the stick shift. They crossed the state line into Oklahoma. The highway was quiet for a Sunday. Folks would be having lunch at this time.

He rolled his shoulders, appreciating the wide-open spaces. "We can stop for lunch whenever you're hungry."

"How far to our destination?"

"Less than an hour." It wouldn't be long until she noticed the hills creeping up on the horizon.

"I can wait."

"That works." She was an easy driving companion. An easy fit in his life. Spending time with Becky was a pleasure. He loved having the opportunity to give her a new experience and show her a unique slice of Oklahoma.

Pete had accompanied him the last time he'd taken this drive. Pete and Emma were swamped with wedding preparations and counting the weeks until Easter Saturday. He and Becky had caught up with the soon-to-be newlyweds over coffee at church this morning, and Emma had mentioned she'd started counting down the days.

Miley now avoided him at church. A big relief. Pete was grateful his family's relations with Miley had improved, and there was less tension. Becky had received Pete and Emma's tick of approval. His friends assumed his close friendship with Becky was moving into relationship territory. They weren't wrong. He wanted them to be right.

Becky gasped and pointed at the windscreen. "Hills. They're real hills."

He shook his head. "I'm glad you're happy."

"I miss hills. You'd understand if you'd seen where I grew up in Sydney. We live in a neighborhood known as the eastern hill in Manly."

"Manly. That's the name of a real place."

"There's a story behind it. If you visit Australia, I'll fill you in."

If he visited. He wanted to visit her homeland after hearing her rave about her home in the beautiful city by the ocean. He'd follow her to the other side of the world, if she loved him.

Love.

The only word that could describe the feelings running through him like a fast-moving stream. If only love was enough. He'd pray love could be enough.

BECKY INHALED SLOW, deep breaths, pacing herself. This was why she avoided the step machine at the gym. Her leg muscles were feeling the uphill workout as she hiked along a trail and staircases leading to the summit at Cathedral Mountain. Sam followed close behind, the trail too narrow for them to walk together.

They'd stopped for lunch in a quiet picnic area in Gloss Mountain State Park, Oklahoma. The brochure she'd collected at the gate entrance had updated her on the park's fascinating history. She'd read the signs and tourist information, intrigued by the plentiful rocks that looked like clear pieces of glass. She could understand why, in the 1800's, the park was known as Glass Mountain. A typographical error was blamed for the name change.

The handrails along the trail came in useful, especially for the rough section of ground leading to the summit. Her hiking boots did their job, keeping her feet steady as she navigated the final steps to flat land at the top.

Sam walked over and reached for her hand. "What do you think?"

She threaded her fingers through his, her tingles from his touch ramping up higher than the summit. "Not what I'd expected. I'd expected trees and greenery, not red dirt and sparse vegetation."

"It's different, for sure."

"And we can see lakes in the distance." She adjusted her base-ball hat, glad she wore jeans and a lightweight long-sleeved t-shirt. A gorgeous spring day. The Cadillac gleamed in the sunshine in the parking lot below.

"I call this place a hidden gem."

"It sure is. Reminds me of the Australian outback." She pulled her phone out of her pocket. "The view is stunning. We need photos."

He let go of her hand. "Go for it. We have time to walk the trails."

"It's so flat up here." No steep peaks like other mountains.

"Watch your step. It's not summer but it's warm enough for rattlers."

"Huh."

"Rattlesnakes."

"Oh." She stepped toward him, clutching his arm. "Are they deadly?"

"They can be. They're noisy and I know what they sound like."

"Have you seen one?"

He nodded. "I'm a farm mechanic, and snakes like warm machinery."

She shivered. "You know first aid, right?"

"Antivenom is what's needed. But yes, I know what to do. I'll keep you safe."

"Ah, my hero." She leaned into his arm, and he tucked his arm around her waist, pulling her closer.

She lifted her phone. "Smile." Selfies were fun. Sam wore his cowboy hat with sunglasses. A good look.

"Did it work?"

She tucked her sunglasses into her shirt pocket, checked the screen, and nodded. "We look good together."

"We are good together." He placed his hand on her cheek.

Another moment. Moment number six, if she hadn't lost count. He wanted to kiss her. She wanted to melt into his arms. Right person. Right place. Romantic location. No Mrs. Alleghany watching or interrupting. Was it the right time?

She spun away, her mind reeling.

"Sam, can you look out for snakes while I take photos?"

He smiled. "Sure."

He walked beside her, maintaining a foot of space between them. She stared out at the flat horizon, her awareness of Sam catapulting in giant leaps to the moon. The tingles had intensified. The sparks couldn't be ignored. She couldn't work side by side with Sam at the play without others noticing their attraction.

Earlier in the week she'd met up with Logan Miles, chatting with him on a bench by the pond. Logan was like a protective big brother, reminding her of Zach. Logan had mentioned the electric atmosphere backstage when she was near Sam. There was nothing fake about her friends-to-more relationship with Sam.

She circled back on the path and reached the trail leading back to the Cadillac.

She turned to Sam. "I'm done."

"Aren't you uploading the photos somewhere?"

She shook her head. "I don't use social media anymore."

"I've never used it. Couldn't see the point."

"You're smart." She stepped closer and looked up, cupping his cheek in her hand. "I've changed my mind."

He pulled off his sunglasses, copying her by tucking his sunglasses into his shirt pocket. "What's changed?"

She stood on tiptoe and removed her cap, looping the back band around her wrist. "I want to kiss you. That is, if you want to kiss–"

Her words were lost. Sam's mouth was on hers, his lips seeking a deeper connection. She grasped his shoulder, appreciating his taut muscles. He wrapped his arm around her waist, drawing her closer, muddling her mind with the tingling sensations that had teased her for weeks.

His cowboy hat blocked the sun, creating a cozy cocoon where she was lost in a maze of unfamiliar feelings. Stronger feelings than she'd known existed. It felt right to be snuggled in his arms and protected from the world. Could they have a future together?

A FEW WEEKS LATER, Becky brewed a pot of green tea and retreated to her dorm room. It was Monday afternoon, and her last week at college before Easter and spring break. Her assignments and essays due this week were completed and submitted.

On Saturday, she'd be Sam's plus-one at Pete and Emma's wedding. A less daunting prospect now she was in a relationship with Sam. She'd started packing for her spring break vacation at the ranch and looked forward to seeing Sam's family, especially his mom.

It was early Tuesday morning in Australia, and Mum was

video calling shortly. Becky poured tea and curled up in her cozy recliner. It was hard to believe there was only one more passion play performance — the Good Friday finale.

The cast and crew wrap-up party was scheduled for Easter Sunday. Sam didn't want to miss the party because it could be his last. They'd go to church, attend the party, and drive to Colorado afterward. Cindy would arrive at the ranch earlier on Easter Saturday.

She sipped her tea and practiced her deep breathing relaxation techniques. The play schedule had kept her busy, and she'd spent most of her spare time with Sam. She'd run out of pre-cooked frozen meals. Her new routine was dinner with Sam and Cindy in the cafeteria. When the menu wasn't appealing, they ate at a restaurant in town.

The awkward moment had happened. Cindy had caught Becky kissing Sam one evening outside the dorm. Her dear friend was thrilled that Becky was dating her cousin for real. Cindy had claimed matchmaker of the year honors and declared her crazy blind date plan an outstanding success.

After their amazing first kiss in Oklahoma, they'd set up kissing rules to manage temptation and allow time for clear thinking about the future. The love words hadn't been spoken, but Sam's actions showed his love louder than any words.

Becky didn't have a plan for June, other than praying for God to make a path clear. Her visa conditions made it difficult for her to stay longer in the States. She missed home. Missed her family. Missed the ocean and the convenience of city living. Time apart would help them make wise decisions on how they could make their relationship work.

Last week, the paparazzi had ramped up their surveillance of Logan. His doubles were helping, but they were outnumbered by photographers. It was too risky for Becky to meet Logan in-person at the petting zoo or the pond. They'd found a few places inside the auditorium and backstage where the public weren't allowed. Privacy wasn't guaranteed, and there was gossip flying around that Logan had a secret love interest.

Her phone buzzed and she connected the video call. "Hey, Mum."

"My sweet girl, it's so good to see your smiling face. How's everything going with Sam?"

"Pretty good. We're busy with the play and haven't made any plans."

"Taking things slow is a good idea. You want to be sure he's the one before you turn your life upside down."

She nodded. "I'm praying, Mum. You know that, right?"

"I'm praying, too. Relationships aren't easy. Love sometimes isn't enough."

"Don't say that, Mum. It's depressing."

"It's also real life. Stuff happens. The test of any relationship is how you manage the problems that are guaranteed to come your way."

"That's fair." She wanted to float along in her little love bubble and not think about what could go wrong.

"Anyway, Mel is here and she wants to talk to you about something. I'll make coffee and be back after Mel's finished."

"Sure." She pressed her lips together, an uneasy feeling gathering steam in her abdomen. Mel hadn't messaged her about wanting to talk, which was unusual.

Mel's face filled the screen. "Hey, lil sis. Are you alone?"

She nodded. "In my room. Door closed. You're worrying me."

"To be honest, I'm worried about you. I have a bad feeling…"

"About what? Tell me."

"It could be nothing, but it's about Jarrod."

"Jarrod." His name left a sour and bitter taste in her mouth. "Have you heard from him?"

Mel nodded. "After church on Sunday. He was alone. Waiting outside the church when the service ended."

"Whoa. I didn't know he was living near Manly."

"He's not. I checked his socials. He's still being seen on the other side of town."

The city and eastern suburbs were Jarrod's home turf. "Then why was he outside our church?" He'd attended services with her until they broke up. Then he'd disappeared and stopped faking an interest in church.

"I think it's about you. He asked questions. Wanted to know where you are."

She inhaled a sharp breath. "What did you say?"

"Nothing." Mel scrunched her face. "It was creepy."

Ugh. "He is creepy." She shoved aside bad memories.

"A group of girls recognized him and wanted selfies."

Jarrod would lap up their attention and tell them to share the pics online. "Nothing's changed."

"Except it has." Her sister frowned. "He was looking for Kelly."

Why Kelly? She was the easiest person on the planet to find online. "She's in Asia somewhere. Bali. Phuket."

"Japan. She posted photos on Saturday. He's not really looking for Kelly."

Becky nodded. "Does Kelly keep in touch with Jarrod?"

Mel sighed and rubbed her hand over her face. "They have mutual friends. That's all I know. Kelly is secretive."

"True." Their sister kept her friends and relationships away from the family. Mum didn't approve. She called Kelly her problem child. Mum wasn't wrong.

"But Kelly contacted me last night. She was concerned about you."

"Me. What? Why?" She loved Kelly, despite her sister being self-absorbed. If Kelly was concerned, there was a problem.

"Kelly and I both got the same message from one of Jarrod's official accounts. He wanted to know where you're living in the States."

Her grip tightened on her phone. "He knows I'm in the States. How?" He could be guessing. Lots of Aussies visited America.

"Did you know there have been stories in the press about Logan being in Gilead?"

"It's the talk of the town." She'd seen the Logan Miles fans wandering around Gilead, desperate to catch a glimpse of their Hollywood hero.

"It's not big news here, but I've seen the stories. His mystery love interest has supposedly been spotted in Gilead."

"Mel, there is no love interest." Logan had assumed the relationship speculation was based on his history of being seen with bikini-clad women. Fair call.

"I believe you. But something is brewing that's connected to you. Kelly's friends have asked her if you're getting back together with Jarrod."

"What? No. That's insane." People and idle gossip. How could Logan stand being a celebrity and subjected to privacy intrusions?

"I know." Mel sipped her coffee. "That's why Kelly's worried about you."

She ran her fingers through her hair. Her uneasy feeling had intensified. "Please pray for me and Sam. And Logan."

"I'm on my knees, lil sis. Stay strong and cling to Jesus."

"That's the plan." One more performance. Then Logan could leave Gilead and take the paparazzi circus with him. Crazy theories were flying around online about why Logan had taken on the role of Judas. She prayed for Logan. Prayed he could stand firm. Prayed he'd find the right time to share his love for Jesus with the world.

CHAPTER 12

On Maundy Thursday, Sam joined the coffee line in Heavenly Brew. A long line, even this early in the morning, now the town bustled with tourists. One more performance, and the passion play was wrapped for another year. His last year.

He'd spoken with Pete about listing his Gilead home for sale after Pete and Emma returned from their honeymoon. Pete's family's realty business was one of the best in town, but Sam couldn't stomach the idea of Matt and Miley selling his house... the home he'd purchased with Miley in mind, back when they were dating.

A guy who looked like Logan Miles was lined up ahead. People were pointing and whispering. Logan had mentioned he had doubles in town — plausible explanation for the simultaneous multiple Logan sightings that had confused the crew. Who'd want to be famous? The guy didn't get a moment's peace. Last Friday, Sam had assisted in evicting an unauthorized photographer from the backstage area.

He shuffled forward in line, thankful he'd scheduled short workdays for today and tomorrow. Then vacation time in Colorado.

Mom had thrived at the ranch. Her blood pressure, anxiety, and insomnia had improved. A few weeks away from work and Dad had made a difference. Sam wasn't sure what that meant for their marriage.

Dad had moped around by himself at home, and no-showed yesterday when Sam had invited him to visit Gilead. They'd lined up a visit for this afternoon to work on Sam's '68 Chevy.

Sam had refused to drive Dad to the ranch on Sunday. Stood firm on that decision. He didn't have time to make a two-hour detour with Becky after the cast and crew party, and still arrive at the ranch in time for Easter Sunday dinner. A family dinner that was important to Mom.

Dad needed to prove to Mom that he was willing to compromise and work on their marriage. Dad taking the initiative and driving to Colorado would be a positive step. Sam prayed his parents would put in the effort. He'd heard both sides of the story, and his loyalties were divided. Not a fun situation.

Sam placed his coffee order and joined the group in the waiting area. He smiled and nodded at familiar faces. Becky had visited earlier during her walk and collected her morning coffee. She'd changed her routine to avoid being delayed by the morning rush.

His name was called and he collected his coffee. He reached for the door handle at the exit.

"Sam. Wait."

He groaned. Mrs. Alleghany. Why would she want to see him? He turned around.

Mrs. Alleghany smiled. "Can we talk outside?"

"Sure." He opened the door, the cowbell clanging as they walked through to the sidewalk.

"Sam, there's something I need to show you." She walked past the neon Heavenly Brew open sign in the window.

He followed and put his coffee on a nearby shop window ledge. This was weird. Mrs. Alleghany's usual way of communicating was to fake whisper gossip loud enough for others nearby to eavesdrop.

"It's about Becky." Mrs. Alleghany handed over her phone. "She's not who you think she is."

What? He scanned the phone screen, scrolling down, his stomach churning acid. No. This must be a fake fan site. He checked the URL in the menu bar. An online international news site with an Australian division.

He placed Mrs. Alleghany's phone beside his coffee, retrieved his phone from his pocket, and typed in the URL. "How did you find this?"

"Quite by accident. Yesterday, a nice man who buys coffee here and takes photographs, told me to search for Logan Miles on this site this morning."

Oh no. Mrs. Alleghany's curiosity would lead her to the gossip site with minimal prompting. The Australian news site headline was in bold capital letters, like an online billboard screaming at him.

LOGAN MILES HIDING WITH SECRET FIANCEE.

Sam enlarged the lead photo on his phone screen. Becky and Logan. Or a Logan lookalike. Sam recognized the campus pond and the park bench where he'd chatted with Becky. He recognized Becky's clothing and baseball cap from her morning walks.

There were more photos. Wait. Was that the Sydney Harbour Bridge in the background? He scanned through a dozen photos connected to the article, his heart thumping harder than a jackhammer.

Mrs. Alleghany clucked like a cranky hen rounding up her chicks. "I can't believe it, Sam. Your Becky. She has a secret life."

He shoved his phone in his pocket and picked up his coffee. "Gotta go. Have a good Easter."

"You, too." Mrs. Alleghany picked up her phone. "Goodbye."

Sam crossed the road, leaving Mrs. Alleghany to cluck on her own. He hopped inside his truck and switched on the engine. He needed to think. He drove a few blocks and turned onto a quiet side street, then parked under a tree and picked up his phone.

The article was there. In technicolor. It wasn't a bad dream. Mrs. Alleghany wasn't making up crazy stories.

He read the text. Twice. Drank coffee. Prayed. He snapped half a dozen screenshots and saved all the individual photos from the article in his phone.

Becky and Logan. Or Bek. Bek was her name in the article. A name she sometimes used when ordering coffee from Letty. He'd figured Becky had shortened her name during peak times to make it easier for Letty, who wrote everyone's names on the takeout cups.

It looked like Becky was known as Bek in Australia. Becky had known Logan in Australia. How was that possible?

The photos looked legit. According to the article, Becky had cheated on a guy called Jarrod, an Aussie actor who was Logan's friend. She'd had a torrid love affair with Logan behind Jarrod's back. Becky had dumped Jarrod and, months later, created a secret love nest hideaway in Kansas. The article implied Logan and Becky were living together in Gilead.

Sam closed his eyes, frowning. The story didn't make sense. Becky didn't sleep anywhere other than in her dorm. There were rules governing the dorms. Cindy would have opened her big mouth and said something if Becky was ever missing at night.

And Logan had never planned to be in Kansas. He'd volunteered to fill in for Leo at the last minute. Leo's unexpected accident was the only reason Logan had participated in the play.

AND BECKY. He'd seen her genuine surprise when she'd first met Logan at the rehearsal. Sam had watched Logan watch Becky, but not in a creepy way. Logan had been supportive and had encouraged Sam to pursue a relationship with Becky. It didn't make sense. Becky wasn't like the other girls who'd sought Logan's attention.

Something was off. The gossip story had more holes than Swiss cheese. But the photos. They looked real. They were from Sydney and someplace called Byron Bay. And Cindy had said Logan's last movie had been filmed in Australia.

Sam downed his coffee dregs, swallowing the hard and horrible truth. Becky had hidden her past connection with Logan. Hidden her meetings with Logan in Gilead. Sam had only seen them talking a couple of times, and only ever at the play.

Would Becky secretly see Logan at the same time she was pretending to be in a fake relationship with Sam? She wouldn't have been cheating on Sam. Not technically. The fake relationship was a mistake. They'd fixed the mistake by making it real, but now he had doubts and regrets.

He messaged Becky and Cindy, canceling dinner plans for tonight. He'd see Becky tomorrow and take time out to pray and think.

Miley had started seeing Matt before she'd dumped Sam. He'd found out later from Pete that Miley had been looking to replace Sam, to discard him like an unwanted old toy. He'd been blindsided by Miley. More doubts plagued his mind. How well did he know Becky? Could he trust her?

BECKY WALKED along the hall toward her next class that commenced in five minutes. Only two days of classes before spring break. Good Friday was tomorrow, and a public holiday in Australia. She'd discovered that Easter in the States was different to home.

Sam had sent her and Cindy a message earlier today, canceling their dinner plans for tonight. Cindy suspected Sam's message was connected to his father. Sam's dad had failed to visit him in Gilead yesterday afternoon.

Becky prayed Sam's parents could reconcile this weekend at the ranch. Her parents' marriage had always been solid. She couldn't imagine the turmoil Sam was experiencing, being an only child and in the middle of the marital mess.

Her phone beeped and she checked her messages. Logan. He wanted to meet her in twenty minutes.

She paused and pressed her lips together. Why couldn't Logan wait until her lunch break? He knew her class schedule. She'd have to cut class to meet him. It should be okay, considering it was her last class before spring break.

She headed for the exit, feeling like a naughty high school student sneaking off campus. Logan had sent her a list of instructions. Detailed instructions, including what to wear and to remove all visible jewelry. That was odd. Why did her appearance matter?

The paparazzi were around. Photographers and Logan fans had descended on Gilead like a plague. A meeting at the pond, one of their main meeting places, was risky.

Within ten minutes she'd changed in her dorm and found the right baseball cap and sunglasses. She'd make it to the pond on time without needing to jog. Would it matter if she was late?

Becky approached the pond and spotted Logan in his usual position on the bench seat.

She sat on the bench and turned to him. "What's up?"

Logan's eyes were hidden behind sunglasses. "A lot. Don't remove your sunglasses or hat."

"Okay." A normal request. She drew in a shaky breath. Logan looked relaxed, but she'd heard hints of tension in his voice. Something was wrong.

"Have you seen any news from Australia today?"

She shook her head.

"I want you to look up a URL. Take screenshots of the whole article and save the photos."

"Sure." She typed the news site URL into her phone and covered her mouth with her hand. No. That headline and photo was wrong. Logan was not her secret fiancé. Gossip garbage. The whole article was a dumpster truck of lies.

She read the lies, refusing to cry. Or laugh at the insanity of the claims. She understood Logan's no jewelry instructions and placed her hands on her knees. Her bare fingers and fingernails that needed a manicure were on display for hidden photographers who could zoom in with their cameras.

One day, this might be a funny memory. Right now, it was her living nightmare.

She saved the screenshots and photos and turned toward Logan. "How? Why? Can we talk here?"

"We can relax. We're recreating one of the article photos. The paps can't make money from selling the same photo."

"I guess so. I'm trying to process what's happening."

He nodded. "The source is Australia. Probably Sydney. My people are on it."

"When did the article drop?"

"At eight this morning, Gilead time."

"Overnight in Australia."

"That's right. My people found it quickly. We're killing the story."

"Is it only one article? I'm offline, and my social accounts are set to private."

"You're not online anywhere?"

She shook her head. "Not since I moved here last year."

"That's a blessing. The trolls won't be able to harass you."

"Okay." She hadn't considered how Logan's followers might react to this news. "How do your people handle this?" What if Sam or Cindy found the article?

"We have good relationships with key people who can shut down false stories."

"That's comforting."

"It really is. Everyone in Gilead knows I never planned to be here. Leo's accident wasn't planned."

"True." She blew out a long breath. "You've been followed for weeks, and I live in a dorm full of people. I don't even know where you live."

"Which means you can answer truthfully if someone asks."

"Will they ask? Or will people assume it's a made-up story because it's obviously wrong?"

He shrugged. "Small towns protect their own. Sam's well known here. Everyone is used to seeing you with Sam."

"Good point."

"Plus people wouldn't guess we know each other."

"Except for the photos. We weren't hiding behind hats and sunglasses in Australia. They cut Jarrod out of the photos."

His frown deepened. "It's possible Jarrod's the source."

She gasped. "No. Surely he wouldn't stoop this low and make up more lies."

"Think about it, Becky. Jarrod's in Sydney. He's not in any photos. The article makes him look like the good guy when we both know he cheated on you."

She nodded. It was suspicious. Mel's warning lingered in her mind. Jarrod's interest in her location might be a clue. She updated Logan on her conversations with Mel.

"I'm sorry Jarrod cheated." His voice held compassion. "I didn't know the details until we started digging for this story."

She blinked. "It was hard." Jarrod's betrayal was like a raw wound that wouldn't heal.

"I'd hold your hand and give you a hug if there weren't cameras around."

"I know." His life was complicated. Someone would be watching them. "I moved countries to get a fresh start." Except her past had caught up with her in spectacular fashion. Now a new list of lies needed to be countered with facts.

"I'm sorry to drag you into this."

"It's okay." She was a survivor. If she could survive Jarrod, she could survive anything. "Will people believe we're only friends?"

"The people who matter will believe us. Everyone else?" He shrugged. "It's outside our control."

"What do we do?" There had to be something she could do to make this situation right.

"Nothing until we confirm the source. I've got interviews and articles lined up for next week when I return to LA."

"Wasn't your original plan to tell the world about your faith next week?"

"Yeah. The good people in Gilead don't need any more annoying media disrupting their town. It's easier to control the narrative from home."

"That makes sense."

He stood. "Please wait here for twenty minutes. The paps should be gone by then. Take care."

"Okay." She'd struggle to cope with his celebrity fishbowl lifestyle and the constant intrusions on his privacy.

He glanced at his phone. "I'll keep you updated. Call me if you need me."

"Will do."

Logan jogged back along the path toward town. Three people emerged from behind trees and bushes, holding cameras and tracking Logan.

Becky leaned back in her seat, a headache brewing. Sam canceling dinner was good timing. She wasn't ready to talk about Logan and the stupid fake news story. Once Logan had killed the story and publicly shared his faith, then she could open up and tell Sam the whole sorry saga. Go horse riding and take her time unpacking why she'd run away to Gilead. Swallow her pride and own her past mistakes.

She loved Sam. He deserved to hear the truth.

She prayed Sam would listen and believe her. Her remaining morning classes were a blur. She met Cindy for lunch in the cafeteria and tried to focus on their conversation. Tried to forget about Logan.

Zach sent her a message. What did her brother want? She opened the message. A video call with their parents. ASAP.

She left Cindy in the cafeteria and returned to her dorm, each step full of dread. A text from Logan arrived, confirming Jarrod was the unnamed source.

She made a mug of hot chamomile tea, the familiar scent with a wisp of vanilla failing to calm her nerves. Jarrod's lucrative revenge plan was outlined in Logan's text. She'd almost gagged at the eye-watering sum Jarrod was paid to sell her out.

Becky curled up in her comfortable chair and hugged a pillow. A tissue box was beside her mug of tea. She wasn't going to cry. She'd already shed enough tears over Jarrod's betrayal.

She connected the video call and Zach answered.

"Hey, Bek. You know why we're calling, right?"

"Logan Miles. You know it's not true."

"Yeah. Dad and Mum are here."

She said hello and appreciated the concern on their faces and in their voices.

Dad cleared his throat. "Can you tell us what happened?"

She nodded. Mum's eyes widened and mouth gaped as Becky provided the summary version of her friendship with Logan.

"Bek, what were you thinking?" Mum shook her head. "Logan is too famous for you to expect any meetings to stay secret."

"I know that now. How did you find the story?"

"Mel." Mum drank from her favorite coffee mug. "I've no idea why she's following Logan and reading gossip."

She nodded and stayed quiet. Mel had kept their conversations secret.

Mum moved out of camera range. "I'll leave you all to sort this out. Call me if you need anything."

"Sure, Mum. We can talk on Sunday night. Aussie time. I'll be at a wedding here on Saturday."

"That works. Love you. Chat later." Mum left the room.

Becky sipped her tea. Dad's face was red. His ears were red. He had his red cranky pants on and pulled up to neck level. She prepared for Dad's wrath to spill.

Dad pointed at her through the phone. "I'll call my lawyer friend next. Get the story removed."

"That's already happening. Logan's people are working on it."

"I assume you have Logan's number," Dad said.

She nodded.

"Can you please send Logan my number and ask his people to call me?"

"Why? What will that achieve?"

Dad's frown deepened the grooves in his cheeks. "Our defamation laws are different to the States. My lawyer can investigate what we can do legally to pull the story and get an apology published."

"Okay, and thanks. Setting the record straight would be helpful."

"That's the plan." Dad turned to Zach. "I'm needed at the hospital. Can you talk to Bek and see if she remembers anything useful about that piece of scum she used to date?"

"Dad, I'm right here." Jarrod was a piece of scum, but hearing Dad say it aloud...

"You take care and stay out of trouble. I'll be in touch." Dad left the room. Thud. The door banged behind him.

Zach rubbed his hands over his face. "We need to talk about Jarrod."

"It's Mel who knows more about Jarrod."

"Huh." Her brother narrowed his eyes. "How's that possible?"

Becky filled him in on her conversations with Mel.

"Wow. Jarrod is a piece of work. Who would be his source in Gilead?"

"I don't think he has a source. Everyone in town knows I live on campus."

"How would he know enough to get paid that outrageous amount of money?"

"Educated guesses based on Gilead gossip and Logan's past behavior around women."

"Why are you spending time with Logan when you're interested in Sam?"

Good question. "By next week, the world will know Logan is a Christian. He's turned his life around and we've become friends."

"Wow. I didn't see that coming."

She nodded. "It's a remarkable story of God's saving grace and Logan's commitment to sobriety."

"Jarrod missed the memo and he's way off base."

"I know. But it's Logan's story to tell, not mine."

"What about Sam? How's he coping with all the drama?"

She sipped her tea, the mug warming her hands. "He doesn't know."

"What? Why?"

"I promised Logan I'd keep his secret."

"There is no secret. The story is out there and you're front and center."

She closed her eyes. "I can't, Zach. Not yet."

"I'm not following. What's going on?"

"I can't tell Sam about Jarrod. It's too soon." Their romantic relationship was too new and precious to pollute with her past mistakes. Jarrod had conned her. She was the naïve idiot who'd thought she knew best. The idiot who'd ignored her sister and others who'd questioned her decision to get involved with Jarrod.

"The secret is out in the wild. You're exposed, and someone will tell Sam about the article."

"Not if Logan and Dad can kill it off fast."

Her brother shook his head. "Billie had a secret that caused trouble in our relationship. You were there, at my birthday party, when everything started to unravel."

"But Billie's secret was different."

"True, but there was still a big fallout. I had trouble navigating the situation. It worked out in the end, but it was hard work to get there."

Her lower lip trembled. Tears hovered, threatening to spill through her lashes. "What if Sam rejects me when he finds out about Jarrod?"

"What if Sam hears about the Logan situation from someone else?"

"That shouldn't happen. No one on campus said anything this morning. Not even the Logan fans."

"How are you going to explain sneaking around with Logan behind Sam's back? Can you explain how you knew Logan in Australia?"

She reached for a tissue and blew her nose. "I don't know. I don't want to think about it."

"You're not a kid anymore. These types of problems can't be ignored."

She couldn't talk to Sam. Couldn't risk exposing her selfishness and stupidity. It was because she cared too much, was too invested, that she needed more time. She prayed Sam wouldn't hear about the Logan situation until she was ready to share her side of the Jarrod story.

CHAPTER 13

The following evening, Sam sat across the table from Becky and Cindy in the cafeteria. Fish was on the Good Friday dinner menu. He ate his serving of battered fish and chips, listening to the girls chat about inconsequential things.

He couldn't work out what was going on in Becky's head. She must know about the Logan story. Mrs. Alleghany couldn't keep her mouth shut on boring gossip, let alone juicy gossip.

No one else seemed to know anything about the story — unless they were too polite to say anything in front of him. The link to the Australian news site was gone. He'd searched online for the story and drawn a blank.

The story was fake, but the photos were real. The pond. The petting zoo. He recognized the Gilead locations. It was plausible that Becky and Logan were friends.

He was puzzled by the Australian photos. Two different locations that were hundreds of miles apart. It had to be more than a coincidence.

He'd given Becky time to bring up the Logan topic. Last weekend, Logan had told Sam he was heading home to California on Easter Saturday.

Sam dived in and interrupted the girls' conversation about their upcoming ranch vacation. "Becky, are you having dessert?"

She shook her head. "I'm full from fish and fries."

"Fish and chips," Cindy said.

"Nope." Becky continued shaking her head. "They're fries, using your logic. If burgers go with fries, then fish should, too."

"You're weird." Cindy sipped her water.

"But you still love me. When you visit Australia, we'll have hot chips at the beach."

Cindy chuckled. "I want to visit the beach near your home."

"Getting back to dessert." He switched his attention to Becky. "If you're skipping dessert, can we go for a walk before we're needed at the auditorium?"

"Sure. It's not as cold outside tonight."

Cindy stood. "Ooh I'd better leave you lovebirds and head back to the dorm."

"Will you be at the play?" Becky asked.

"Of course." Cindy put her empty plate on a tray. "I have a ticket near the front. Good Friday is always the best performance."

He nodded. "It's the day for it."

Becky smiled. "It sure is."

He helped the girls clear the table and walked with Becky toward the exit.

She reached for his hand, threading her fingertips through his.

A lump formed in his throat. The Logan secret was driving him crazy. How could he bring up the subject and encourage her to talk?

"I'm glad I can wear sneakers at the play," she said.

"Me too." The comfortable sneakers he wore were his usual walking shoes.

"I can't believe tonight is the finale."

"Yup. My final show after seven years." Huge gulp. He'd miss working with the crew next year.

"Moving to the ranch is a big change."

"A good change." Irrespective of what happened with Becky and his parents, he'd made the firm decision to relocate from Gilead to the ranch.

They walked in silence. His frustration escalated another notch. He had no choice but to raise the subject himself.

"Becky, I have a question."

"Sure. What's up?"

He slowed his pace. "When were you going to tell me about the Logan secret engagement story?"

She gasped. "How did you hear?"

"Mrs. Alleghany. Yesterday morning."

"Oh." She let go of his hand and crossed her arms across her body.

"What's the deal?"

She kept walking, head down. "It's complicated."

Was that all she had? He counted to twenty. Silence. "And what does that mean?"

She looked away, her body language rejecting his attempts to continue the conversation.

He took a deep breath. And another deep breath. Kept walking. Becky's rejection was like a beesting that would fester over time.

Miley had behaved in the same way when Sam had confronted her about Matt. Miley had shut down. Refused to talk. Didn't defend herself. Didn't attack him. Didn't engage.

"I can't do this, Becky."

She stopped walking, swinging around to stare at his feet. "Do what?"

"This. The silent treatment."

She kicked a stone off the path. "I can't talk."

"Why?"

"I just can't, okay."

"Here's the thing." He kept his voice soft and calm. "We're in a relationship together. Open and honest communication is a deal-breaker."

"What are you saying?"

"I can't be in a relationship where the other person shuts down and puts me in the freezer." Miley had strung him along for months. Made empty promises that she'd talk soon and tell him what's going on. Her lies had broken his trust and revealed the truth about her selfishness.

Becky looked up, her face downcast. "What do you want to know?"

Where to start? At least she was talking. "Have you been meeting Logan in Gilead?"

She nodded. "We're friends. Nothing more."

"I believe you, Becky. Did you first meet Logan in Australia?"

"Yep. We knew the same people."

"Okay." A good starting point. "Did you date Logan in Australia?"

"No. never. I'm not interested in Logan. You have to believe me."

"I do." It was a relief that he did believe her. He liked Logan. Sam was glad that Logan hadn't been involved with Becky. "What else do I need to believe?"

"I can't talk about Australia."

"Can't or won't?"

"Both. Some of it's not my story to tell." She wrapped her arms around her torso and stared at the ground. "I left Bek behind in Australia. Started over as Becky." Her tone was low and firm. "I never intended to meet you or anyone."

He'd hit a wall. "But you did meet me. And that was good."

She nodded. "We should go to the auditorium."

Subject closed. He couldn't do this again. Dad had stonewalled Mom's attempts to negotiate a compromise. Sam had learned the core issue at the heart of his parents' relationship problems was poor communication.

"Before we go." He stopped walking. Bright oranges and pinks lit up the sky. His hopes and dreams were fading like the sunset.

She turned to him. "I'm listening."

"I don't find it easy to talk about past hurts. Miley is a difficult topic."

"I can relate."

"Just because it's hard doesn't mean we should avoid it."

"That's fair." She uncrossed her arms and stepped toward him. "I don't want to fight."

He softened his tone. "That's why we need to talk. Poor communication is a big problem in my parents' marriage."

"I'm sorry to hear that. It's a hard situation."

"It sure is." He held her gaze. "Effective communication requires effort from everyone in the relationship."

"That makes sense."

He nodded. "I already have one failed long-distance relationship behind me. If we want a future together, we'll soon be spending time apart. We need to believe we can trust each other."

She folded her arms across her torso and looked away. "I can't talk about this now."

Back to shutdown mode, the loop she wasn't willing to break. If they couldn't talk now, how would they manage when they lived on opposite sides of the world?

He stepped toward her. "When can we talk?" His question hung between them in the light breeze.

She stepped back, looked past his shoulder. "At the ranch. There's stuff I need to pray about and process first."

His heart cracked around the edges, her words like a knife blade piercing the outer layer. He let it bleed, choosing not to rationalize or sugarcoat her words. Accepted the truth. Braced himself for rejection. His love might not be enough.

~

BECKY STRODE into the auditorium lobby with Sam and they parted ways. A perfect metaphor that illustrated how she'd botched their after-dinner conversation. Sam had known about the fake news article for two days and said nothing.

The bigger problem was she'd said nothing.

As she joined a short line for the restroom, Zach's words of warning lingered in her mind. She'd ignored her brother, believing she knew better. She'd make an idiot look smart. Jarrod's appalling attack on her integrity would take time to process. She needed a clearer head before sharing her angst with Sam.

Sam deserved someone better than her. He'd been conned by Miley. Becky had been conned by Jarrod. The difference was in the details. Miley had moved on with the man she'd soon marry. Jarrod had cheated on Becky with multiple women, casual relationships that had nothing to do with commitment and marriage.

Jarrod's role in the Logan news story had wounded her. The blatant lies and public slurs on her character had cut deep. Jarrod must love money and hate her in equal measure. He'd validated her decision to study in Kansas and escape from his world.

Her therapist had kept her file open, just in case the Jarrod situation blew up before Becky returned to Australia. She'd book an appointment next week, when the pressure and her stress levels were lower, and she'd had an opportunity to discuss the situation with Sam.

She used the restroom and checked the time. Sam needed her backstage in fifteen minutes. She could hide somewhere or be brave. Decisions.

"Becky."

She recognized Logan's voice and spun around. He wore a black scarf that covered his head and beard.

"Hey."

"Are you okay?" Concern shone in his eyes.

"Not really. I've messed up everything with Sam."

"He knows?"

She nodded. "But not from me."

"Follow me. There's an empty wardrobe storage room. We can talk there."

"Okay." She walked behind Logan, keeping five steps behind him as they wove around groups of people.

He stopped in front of a door. Opened it. Stepped inside, leaving it ajar.

She waited a couple of minutes and slipped through the door, closing it behind her.

He sat in a plastic chair beside an old clothing rail. "What's happening?"

She sat opposite, appreciating the empathy in his eyes. "I'm gonna cry and mess up my makeup."

"Waterproof mascara."

She nodded and sniffed.

"You'll be fine." He grinned. "I know how to fix makeup disasters."

A smile tugged at her lips. Logan the makeup artist to the rescue. "I feel better already."

"Is Sam okay?"

She let out a long sigh. "I'm frustrating him because I can't talk."

"Talk about what?"

"The situation. My sisters can talk and cry and talk some more when something goes wrong. I can cry, but I can't talk until I process."

He nodded. "We're talking about Jarrod."

"Unfortunately. He's trying to ruin my life."

Logan leaned forward on his elbows, his fingers steepled under his chin. "That might be short-lived. I have good news."

"Tell me." She needed good news.

"My people contacted your dad and his lawyer." He held her gaze. "You didn't mention your dad's friend is a top Sydney lawyer."

She shrugged. "Dad's a surgeon who plays a lot of golf."

"That figures. My people were impressed. We've taken legal action in Australia to correct the Jarrod situation. You won't hear from Jarrod again."

"Thank you. That's good news."

"Thank your dad's lawyer. He got the story pulled in Australia. We blocked it from being published in the States."

"That's a relief." Her anxiety levels dropped a little lower.

He nodded. "My doubles have been on a public relations mission. They're spreading the word that the Australian article was fake news. Next week, the world will know the real story about my time in Gilead."

"Oh, wow. That explains why no one has said anything."

"And the lady who gossips in Heavenly Brew—"

"You mean Mrs. Alleghany."

"That's her. A few hours ago she identified the reporter who'd tipped her off about the story. We're working on that lead."

She widened her eyes. "What? Someone used Mrs. Alleghany to spread fake news."

"It appears so, although Mrs. Alleghany is unlikely to join the dots. She had good intentions."

"That sounds about right." Poor Mrs. Alleghany. If she only knew her role in the chaos, she'd be sharing her version of the story with the world.

"Don't give up on Sam. He loves you. You love him. It's only geography you need to overcome."

"Thanks, Logan. How can I thank you?"

His grin matched the sparkle in his warm eyes. "Your friendship has kept me sane. Stay in touch. And I'll expect an invite to your wedding."

"Will do." She checked the time on her phone. "Pray there is a wedding. Catch you later." She left Logan in the pokey room and headed to her usual position backstage. Emotion choked her throat. The cast and crew were like a big family, and she'd miss being involved with the play.

Sam nodded. "I thought you'd lost your way."

Lost her way? Perhaps she had. Facts. In many ways she'd lost her focus on Jesus. Lost sight of the big picture. Lost sight of the biblical truths she should cling to during a crisis.

"I'm here now." She accepted the bottle of water Sam had collected on her behalf. This man. In little ways, he did big things. "I detoured to chat with Logan."

"Is he okay?"

"He's doing fine. He updated me on the situation in Australia."

"The situation you don't want to talk about." His mouth flattened in the direction of a frown, the only clue that Sam wasn't happy.

"Can we talk at the ranch?" The moment of truth.

"Okay." He glanced at his phone. "We're on. Let's get moving."

His one-word answer gave her hope, deflating her anxiety like a limp balloon. She valued his gift of time.

The performance commenced, and she switched into autopilot, working with Sam to move the props on and off stage. They made a good team. Could their teamwork transition into a lasting marriage?

She could recite many of the actors' lines. She'd watched them give their all and woo the audience. She prayed the audience had eyes and ears open to Jesus. She prayed her own focus would remain on Jesus. Something she'd failed to do after the Logan story had dropped.

Sam was polite, but he was more reserved than usual. He'd taken a mental step back from their relationship, and it was all her fault. She'd pushed him away and had to bear the consequences. She didn't know if she could navigate a future with Sam.

Becky switched her attention to the play. The Good Friday

scenes at Calvary played out on the stage. She let her tears flow. She was broken. She needed salvation. She needed Jesus. She prayed for peace and His timing to work through her issues with Sam.

The performance wrapped and she found a supply of tissues backstage. The crew would start packing up the auditorium tomorrow morning. She wasn't required to attend and looked forward to sleeping in. Mel had messaged her, wanting to talk tonight. She waved goodbye to Sam and walked back to the dorm with Cindy.

Cindy chatted nonstop, unaware of Becky's tense situation with Sam. Becky had dodged the potentially awkward good night kiss moment with Sam outside the dorm. She had the wedding tomorrow. Sam needed her support at the wedding. No time for moping and feeling sorry for herself.

She gravitated to her cozy chair in her room. She was emotionally attached to her recliner. Maybe Sam could take her chair to the ranch when she moved out of the dorm. He could keep it. The thought of moving home was bittersweet. If only she could live in two places at once.

Becky checked the time and called Mel. She wouldn't miss time zone math.

Mel's face filled the screen. "Hey, lil sis. Are you okay?"

"You're sounding like Logan."

Her sister raised her eyebrows. "Does he call you lil sis?"

"No. He asked me tonight if I was okay."

"Were you?"

She shook her head. "I followed him into an empty wardrobe room and we talked."

"Bek! What are you thinking?"

"Huh. What now?"

"Hiding in a closet with Logan where people will assume you're doing anything but talking. Are you trying to kill Dad?"

Her mouth gaped. "Is your rant over?"

Mel nodded. "You can walk into trouble without trying."

"Without thinking is a better description." Her impulsive tendencies might be linked to anxiety. Something to consider in her next therapy session. "I guess I haven't made the best choices."

"You think? Mum is baking. Dad's driving her mad because of you and Kelly."

"What's Kelly done now?" She hadn't heard from Kelly in weeks. No photos. No emails. Not even a one-word reply to her last text message.

"I don't know the details. I think she needs money, but Dad's run out of patience."

"That's fair." At least she'd lived within her budget in Gilead. Not being near a mall helped.

"Back to you, lil sis. Are you sure no one noticed you in a closet with Logan?"

"I'm sure. He wore a scarf over his head and beard. I only recognized him because I know his voice."

"You live dangerously."

"Don't worry. You'll meet Logan at my wedding."

Mel squealed. "What wedding? Have you got a ring?"

"No. Calm the farm. Logan thinks I'll marry Sam."

"What do you think?"

"I don't know. I think I made everything worse tonight." She recapped the situation, talking through the events of the last forty-eight hours.

Mel shook her head. "You know Zach is right. You should have told Sam about Logan and Jarrod yesterday morning."

"The Logan situation is sorted. Sam knows and believes we're only friends. In fact, Sam and Logan could become friends. They get along well."

"Your life is strange."

"But not boring."

"No. Never boring. Have you worked out why Sam is backing off?"

Becky pressed her lips together. "I don't think he trusts me."

"I wouldn't trust you."

"Hey! Don't be mean."

Mel raised her hands. "I'm helping you process. What's mean about that?"

"Sorry." Becky closed her eyes. "Sam's not happy that he didn't find out about Logan from me."

"That's why Zach's right."

"You always side with Zach."

"Zach is almost always right."

"I hate you all." One day she'd be right, and her siblings would be wrong.

Mel snickered. "How would you cope without a big brother and sister to keep you on the straight and narrow?"

"I think you've both failed."

"There's only so much we can do." Her sister shrugged. "It's your life. Your choices."

"I will apologize to Sam."

"You'd better. A real apology. Not just pacifying words."

She straightened her legs, stretching in her recliner. "I don't do that."

"We all do that. I get the impression Sam feels stuff deeply. You wounded him by not talking."

Becky blew out a long sigh. "I'm scared he'll reject me."

"Do you trust him?"

Good question. "We only met in January. I haven't known him long. My past judgment was flawed …"

"Sam isn't Jarrod."

"I know."

"Do you?"

Becky focused on her deep breathing, pondering Mel's words.

"I'll be praying for you, lil sis. I think Sam's worth the risk."

She nodded. Could she open her heart to Sam and risk rejection? Sam wasn't Jarrod. Sam's faith was genuine.

She'd hurt Sam, and making excuses to justify why she was right to stay quiet was not a solution. Did she have the courage to step out in faith and risk her heart being trampled?

CHAPTER 14

The next day, Sam held Becky's hand as they walked back to his truck, only a block from the church. The sun warmed his face and defrosted the chill that had crept into their relationship. They'd parked their issues at the curb and agreed to focus on enjoying Pete and Emma's Easter Saturday wedding.

The late-morning ceremony at their church was heart-warming and faith-filled. The bride and groom had left the church for photos with their bridal party. Now they had time to kill before the luncheon reception at a wedding venue outside town.

Becky let go of his hand and opened her purse. "I knew I'd forgotten something."

"What's missing?"

"My lip gloss. Can we detour via my dorm?"

"Sure." He unlocked his truck, glad he'd spent time cleaning the interior cabin yesterday.

Becky was beautiful in ordinary clothes. Today's wedding outfit of an elegant pink dress and matching heels added a sophistication he found irresistible. Her dark hair flowed loose over her shoulders. She'd drawn plenty of male attention at the church, along with appreciative glances.

Sam appreciated Becky's support and her willingness to be his plus-one despite all the complications. The undercurrents in their relationship were like tiny ripples bubbling beneath the surface. Her mind-blowing beauty didn't change the facts. He wasn't prepared to commit to a long-distance relationship if she wasn't prepared to discuss hard issues.

Within minutes they arrived at the parking lot on campus.

She opened the passenger door. "I won't be long."

"Take your time. Those shoes don't look easy to walk in."

She chuckled. "I used to wear heels all the time. I'll be fine."

"Okay." Her old life in Sydney was worlds apart from Gilead. The life she'd return to in the coming weeks.

He stepped out of his truck, leaving the windows open to catch the breeze. He loosened his tie and stood in the shade of a nearby tree. If only he could roll up the long sleeves of his button-up shirt. He'd ironed out the creases and needed to be presentable for the reception.

His phone beeped in his pocket. He checked the screen. Mom. She wanted to talk ASAP. He dialed her number.

"Mom, what's up?"

"Oh Sam, I don't know what to do with your father."

He groaned. "Isn't he leaving for the ranch now?"

"I tried calling earlier, and he wouldn't answer. He finally picked up and said it's too hard. The drive is too long."

"I'm sorry." Five hours was not an onerous drive for Dad. He'd been making excuses to avoid doing important things. "What can I do?"

"Are you at the reception?"

"Not yet. We'll go there next."

"Can you call him? See if you can find out what's going on, and if he has a good reason for delaying."

He blew out a frustrated breath. They'd planned for Dad to

visit Gilead and help Sam work on the Chevy on Thursday, but Dad had cancelled at the last minute. Was there anything Sam could say that would make a difference? "Okay. I'll try."

"Thank you. I love and appreciate you."

"Love you too, Mom. I'll call back soon."

He ended the call and closed his eyes. *Lord, please help me to have a constructive conversation with Dad.*

He made the call, and Dad surprised him by answering straight away.

"Dad, are you ready to leave for Colorado?"

"I don't think I can do it."

"Why?"

"I slept in, and I have stuff to do."

"What stuff?" He waited for Dad to elaborate.

Becky returned to the truck and waited by the passenger side.

He nodded at Becky. "Dad, are you still there?"

"The house is a mess and laundry needs doing." He sounded like a child making excuses for not finishing their homework.

"Do you have clean clothes for two nights away?"

"Yup."

"Have you packed?"

"Almost done."

Sam unclenched his jaw. They were making progress. "Forget about laundry. Work on tidying the kitchen, putting out the trash, and packing the car."

"That will take time."

Sam swallowed a harsh response. Prayed for patience. "If you leave within the hour, you'll arrive by dinner." Dad was familiar with the route and couldn't claim he'd get lost.

"It's a long drive."

"Stop at the diner and order a cheeseburger. Remember how much we used to love their chocolate shakes?"

"The shakes are good."

"Order a chocolate one, for old times' sake." The diner held fun road trip memories.

"Remember that time you spilled chocolate shake all over your mom's lap?"

"How can I forget? Mom wouldn't order a replacement."

Dad laughed. "You'd already slurped half the shake."

"Yeah, but it was worth a try. Go get ready, and text Mom when you're leaving."

"I'm worried about the drive."

"The hardest part is getting out the door and into the car. Once you're on the road, you'll be alright."

"It's hard, son."

"I know, but Mom needs you to step up. Meet her halfway."

Dad paused, cleared his throat, and took his time answering. "I don't know if I can."

"I believe in you, Dad. I know you love Mom and take your wedding vows seriously."

"I wouldn't cope if your mother left me."

Sam clenched his fist and unclenched it. Could Dad understand Mom's perspective?

He needed a cool head and the right words. "Then you need to drive to Colorado now and talk to her. Show her you love her."

Dad was quiet. Sam prayed he hadn't said too much. Dad's anxiety was high and his motivation levels low. A tricky combination.

"I do love your mother," Dad said.

"I know you do. Show her by driving to Colorado. I'll see you for dinner tomorrow night."

"Will I meet Becky?"

"Yes, and she's waiting for me to drive to the wedding reception."

"Okay. I can do it." Dad's voice held a resolute tone.

Finally. He'd been around and around this merry-go-round

with Dad too many times. It was exhausting. "You can do it, Dad. I'll be praying."

"Thanks, son. I'll contact your mother soon."

"Good plan." Sam ended the call and walked over to Becky.

Her eyebrows were raised. "Is everything okay?"

"Dad's having one of those days."

"Not good."

"Yeah. I just need to call Mom. Five minutes at the most."

"No problem. We won't be late."

He nodded and walked around to the driver's side, then called Mom.

"Sam, your father just sent me a message."

"Good news, I hope."

"He's leaving in twenty minutes."

He let out a relieved breath. "I'm glad. I'll be praying he has a safe trip."

"Thanks. I'm not sure what you said, but thank you."

"You're welcome. I'm looking forward to seeing you tomorrow."

"How are things with Becky?"

Becky was on the other side of his truck, head bent, looking down at her phone. Sunlight filtered through the leaves, highlighting golden strands in her hair. "We need to talk."

"She hasn't talked about Australia?"

"Not yet. I don't know if things will work out."

"I'll be praying for you both."

"Appreciate that. I better go, or we'll be late for the wedding reception."

"Has Miley given you any trouble?" Mom asked.

"Not so far. Our plan is to avoid her."

"Good idea. I'll message you with Dad updates, so you won't worry."

"Thanks. That will be helpful." He ended the call and walked around the truck.

Becky smiled. "Is everything okay?"

"I think so. Dad should be leaving for the ranch soon."

"That's good." She stepped toward him and straightened his tie. "I'm looking forward to meeting him tomorrow."

"All going well, that should happen. We better go." Before Sam decided he'd rather spend the afternoon kissing Becky.

They made good time, arriving at the reception venue five minutes early.

Sam parked his truck and held Becky's hand as they approached the wedding guests gathered in an outdoor courtyard.

"Are you nervous?" she asked.

"I don't like attention." Or wearing suits. The jacket wasn't comfortable. He'd put it over the back of his chair as soon as they were seated indoors.

"No one will be paying attention to us. It's Pete and Emma's day."

"If only." Becky attracted attention wherever she went. Her sweet Australian accent combined with the Logan Miles rumors had put Becky on the Gilead social radar.

Group photos with the family were in progress on the far side of the courtyard. Colorful displays of roses made nice center-pieces on the outdoor tables. He waved to Pete.

"Sam," Pete yelled. "We need you and Becky for photos."

He gave Pete a thumbs-up and turned to Becky. "I told you so."

"Come on." She pulled on his hand. "We don't want to keep the bride waiting."

He followed Becky's lead, weaving around groups of guests in the courtyard and declining drinks from servers.

Pete slapped him on the back. "About time you got here. Let's get these photos done."

"No worries." Sam put his arm around Becky's waist, drawing her close to his side. He'd missed being close to her. The last few days of no kissing had felt like an eternity. He smiled for the photographer, following instructions for multiple photos with the bride and groom.

Becky and Emma whispered and giggled about something. He was glad they were friends.

Pete took a few steps back, away from the camera. "I'd like a few photos of Sam and Becky."

Becky nodded and put her arm around Sam's waist. "Is this right?"

"It sure is." Pete whistled. "You two look good together."

Sam grinned. This moment would be awkward if they were in a fake relationship. His close friends and family were invested in his relationship with Becky and were praying they'd make a long-distance relationship work.

Sam continued to smile for the camera, enjoying having Becky close by his side. He'd left his cowboy hat in the truck, figuring it didn't look right with a tailored suit. Becky had helped him order the suit. He had zero fashion sense, and she had good taste.

The photographer waved them away, moving on to her next victims.

Sam kept his arm around Becky's waist, resisting the strong inclination to kiss her. They headed indoors and found their table toward the back, away from where Miley would be seated with Pete's family.

The bridal party made their grand entrance and appetizers were served. Becky made small talk with the guests at their table. She was a natural with people, and he started to relax. The main course was served and he swapped plates with Becky. She preferred chicken, and he was happy with beef. The speeches were fun, and Matt fulfilled his best man duties with tales from Pete's childhood.

The bride and groom hit the dance floor. Sam draped his arm around the back of Becky's chair. The tables around them emptied as people paired up and joined the bridal party dancing near the front of the room.

She leaned back into his chest, a dreamy smile tilting up her kissable lips. "Would you like to dance?"

"I'd rather stay here and cuddle you." Dancing was not his thing. He had poor coordination — another reason why he was happy to decline being in the bridal party. Pete had told him about their dancing lessons, and how Emma had outclassed him.

"Are you sure?" Becky's gaze roamed his face, settling on his mouth.

"I'm sure." He dropped a kiss on her lips. Just one kiss. One kiss couldn't hurt, right? He'd treasure these moments, and their time together. He'd have the photos from Pete and Emma's wedding photographer to remember this day with Becky.

A loud cough and strong, tangy perfume interrupted his romantic daydreams.

He looked up. Miley glared at him. She wore a skimpy red dress that accentuated her curves, and red lipstick that matched her red-hot anger. A volcanic explosion was imminent.

"You two are looking cozy." Miley patted her blonde hair, styled in a fancy updo.

"What do you want?" He tried, and failed, to keep his voice even.

"Thought I'd stop by and chat." Miley switched her gaze to Becky. "You've been a busy girl."

What was Miley's game? "We've both been busy with the play."

Miley smirked. "Becky, or should I say Bek, has been in a relationship with Logan the hunk."

Becky's eyes narrowed. "That's not true."

"The story was published in an Australian newspaper." Miley's smirk mirrored the triumphant glint in her eyes.

"And unpublished." He glared at Miley. "It's not true."

"But it is." Miley placed her hands on her hips. "I read the article and saw the photos of her and Logan in Australia. I did some more digging, and found articles about her ex. An actor. Jarrod, I think his name is."

Becky held her composure and stared at the ground. She looked like she'd prefer to sink through the floor than participate in a confrontation with Miley.

He'd take Miley on. It was time. Past time. "What Becky did, or didn't do, in Australia is none of your business —"

"It's your business, Sam." Miley lowered her voice, as if she was sharing a dark secret. "She cheated with Logan. Twice. She cheated on you."

He straightened his spine. "You're a hypocrite, Miley. This isn't the time or the place to rehash how you cheated on me."

Miley's face flamed a shade of red darker than her dress. "How dare you —"

"How dare you." He kept his voice low. His anger simmered. "I turned the other cheek and didn't argue when you dumped me for Matt. I know you were seeing Matt before you officially ended our relationship."

Miley puffed out her chest. "I was not —"

"I'm sick of the lies, Miley. You did me a favor when you dumped me. I've moved on, and I'm happy."

Miley wrinkled her nose and switched her attention to Becky. "I can't see how a girl like her would be happy living on a ranch. There's no hot celebrity actors hanging around in the middle of nowhere."

Becky tensed. "I'm going to find the restroom." She shot Miley a defiant look. "Don't follow me."

Miley switched on her fake smile and saccharine tone. "Wouldn't dream of it."

Becky walked away, leaving Sam with his nemesis.

He wanted closure. He needed closure. He stared at Miley. "You have no class."

"She's bad news, Sam." Miley clucked her displeasure. "I found out why she ran away from Australia."

He shook his head. "You don't know anything."

"Mrs. Alleghany showed me the article. Becky will break your heart. She was seen with Logan. Why else would they be hanging out?"

"That's your problem. Don't put your standards on Becky. Just because you'd have an affair with Logan if he so much as looked at you doesn't mean everyone else would."

Miley rolled her eyes. "He's Logan Miles. The Logan Miles. The man is smoking hot."

"He's a man who gets paid a lot of money for his work. He's Becky's friend. He's my friend."

"Sam, are you an idiot? No one in their right mind would say no to a fling with Logan Miles."

He shook his head again. "Have you shared this opinion with your husband? The man you promised to be faithful to when you got married?"

"I'm not talking about me. I'm talking about Becky."

"We're done, Miley. I'm selling my house in Gilead and leaving town for good." He stood. "Have a nice life."

He walked away, heading outdoors. He needed to let off steam and calm down. Miley wasn't worth it. She was his past, and Becky was his future.

Sam checked his phone. Good news from Mom. Dad was on his way to Colorado. *Thank you, Jesus.*

He sent Becky a text, letting her know he was outside. He'd walk and pray and calm his temper. He'd never been more thankful that Miley had dumped him. Their breakup had been hard, and his sympathies were with Pete's brother. Miley was Matt's problem.

~

BECKY CLOSED the restroom door and walked back along the hall toward the reception room. She might hide in the hall if Miley was still with Sam at their table.

Miley was brazen to accuse Becky of being a cheater in front of Sam. A mortifying experience that reminded her of why she'd left Sydney last year. Gossip was horrible. People were horrible. Miley was horrible in how she'd weaponized the article.

How awful of Miley to take the fake news story and create her own version of Becky's relationship history to suit Miley's own twisted narrative. Becky loved Sam for standing up for the truth and calling Miley out. He'd said little about his own history with Miley, other than the reasons for why he'd need a plus-one today. Miley the maneater was on the prowl, and Sam was her target.

Her phone beeped and she checked the screen. Sam. Her pulse slowed. He was outside. She sent him a text and made her way to the courtyard.

He gave her a terse smile. "We can talk in the rose garden."

"Sure." She reached for his hand, linking her fingertips through his. A stroll in the garden would provide privacy.

They walked in silence. Sam seemed lost in thought. She waited for him to initiate a conversation.

"I'm sorry about Miley," he said.

"It's not your fault."

"She attacked you because of me."

She squeezed his hand. "I'm an easy target. Strangers have done this before."

"What? Where?"

"In Sydney. The Logan photos are part of it."

He paused, turning to face her. "I'm not going to push you to talk."

"I know." She closed her eyes for a moment, praying for courage. "Tomorrow. After the party. We can talk on our way to the ranch."

He reached for her other hand. "I'm going to tell you about Miley. It might help you understand why she was mean."

"Okay." She held his gaze, empathizing with the pain in his beautiful eyes.

"I started dating Miley in high school. I was a year older and on the football team."

"The quarterback."

"No. That was Matt. He was a year ahead of me and Pete."

She nodded.

"Miley was a cheerleader. She was popular and chose me." He let go of one hand, running his fingers through his short hair. "I'd thought I was the luckiest guy in the world."

"We think we know everything at that age."

"Yeah. Miley went to college, and we started a long-distance relationship. She came home for holiday weekends and her college breaks. I'd occasionally drive to Illinois to see her."

"She went to college interstate?"

"With Matt."

"Oh, but he's older."

"Matt had a sports scholarship at a different college until he was injured. He changed courses and they ended up at the same college."

She nodded. That made sense.

"Spring break last year, I organized a picnic date at a high school football game. I'd thought she'd appreciate the nostalgia."

"A sweet idea."

"I'd thought so. I'd made the mistake of buying Valentine's chocolates, not knowing she was on a sugar-free diet."

"Ouch. Awkward."

He nodded. "Miley stood me up at the football game. She ignored my texts. I was worried she'd been in an accident or something."

"I can only imagine."

"She texted me the next day, claiming she'd mixed up the

dates. A few weeks later she called me. I was expecting an apology. She dumped me over the phone."

"Oh Sam, that's hard."

He pressed his lips together. "I found out later from Pete, after Matt and Miley got engaged, that Miley had been with Matt on the night of the football game."

Becky sighed. "I'm sorry she cheated on you."

"Yeah, but after Miley's performance tonight, I'm glad she dumped me."

"She's a piece of work."

"But she's in the past. We had a difficult conversation after you left. I can guarantee she'll avoid us."

"That's a relief. I don't want Pete and Emma's wedding ruined by unnecessary drama."

"Agreed. Let's go back inside and have dessert."

"A fabulous idea." She walked with Sam back to the courtyard and inside the reception room as the servers were carrying dessert trays to the tables. Perfect timing.

Becky was determined to put the Miley situation out of her mind. She was confident Sam would understand how and why she'd gotten caught up in the Jarrod mess. She prayed the rest of the wedding would be uneventful.

CHAPTER 15

*B*ecky stifled a yawn and answered the video call from
her family. Six in the morning on Easter Sunday was
too early. She stretched out in her chair, planning to squeeze in a
walk and breakfast before Sam drove her to church.

"Hey, lil sis." Mel's smiling face filled the screen. "You look
wrecked."

"Thanks, and Happy Easter to you. How was dinner?"

"Good. Zach and Billie are here. Kelly's still away."

"What's happening with her?"

"She's supposed to fly home next week."

"Okay." Becky looked forward to catching up with Kelly.

"They're all cleaning up the dinner dishes. We have time to
chat." Mel switched her phone from speaker to her earbuds.
"How was the wedding?"

"Where do I start?" Becky updated Mel on the events of
yesterday, including the horrible conversation with Miley.

Mel gasped. "No. Miley sounds like Jarrod's perfect match."

"She's married, and I got the impression she was jealous of my
supposed love affair with Logan. She'd probably go for Jarrod as
well."

Mel shook her head. "Didn't you say she attends your church?"

She nodded. "Sam had a difficult conversation with Miley. It didn't end well."

"And you had no idea Miley was like this?"

"Not a clue. I'd seen Miley at church. Said hello a couple of times. Emma, who's now Miley's sister-in-law, isn't a Miley fan."

"Emma and Pete would have seen Miley dump Sam and start a relationship with Matt."

"Yeah. Miley cheated on Sam. It was Pete who broke that news to Sam."

"Awkward. What does this mean for your relationship with Sam? Have you told Sam about Jarrod and the Logan connection?"

"I'm doing that later today, when we have hours in the truck with nothing but boring corn fields for company."

Mel chuckled. "What's on your schedule?"

"Church first, then the cast and crew wrap-up party. We'll arrive at the ranch in time for Sam's family dinner."

"Sounds busy," her sister said.

"I'm packed and organized. Cindy's already at the ranch. Sam's dad finally got there last night. We're praying Sam's parents can work out their differences."

"I'll be praying, too. I'm excited that things are looking up for you and Sam."

"Yeah. I appreciate your prayers."

Mel smiled. "The family are here. Give me a sec." She removed her earbuds and switched her phone to speaker, panning out to a wider screen view.

Becky waved and greeted her family. Her heart was full. Zach and Billie were a cute couple, and they were joking around. Mum and Dad looked like they'd gotten over the last few days of stress. Dad's face was a normal tone and the stress lines between his eyebrows were less prominent.

Becky clapped her hands together. "I have an announcement."

Mom grinned. "Can I start planning a wedding?"

She laughed. "Not yet. I think Sam and I can find a way to make a long-distance relationship work."

"Woo-hoo." Zach hi-fived her through the phone screen. "I can't wait to meet Sam."

"All in good time. I'd appreciate prayers that we can work out the details."

"Are you still flying home in June?" Mom asked.

She nodded. "We've only known each other for a few months. I don't want to rush into anything."

"That's sensible," Dad said. "I'm proud of how you've handled the Jarrod mess."

Billie squealed. "I can't believe you're friends with Logan Miles. How cool is that!"

"He wants a wedding invite," Mel said.

Billie jumped up and down. "We'll get to meet him. Bek, you have to marry Sam!"

Her family laughed.

Zach shot his wife a warm look. "Don't you get any ideas and run off with him!"

"You silly man. I love you." Billie leaped into her husband's arms.

Her brother kissed his wife, shutting down any further Logan fangirling.

Becky's heart melted. Zach and Billie were her marriage role models. She wanted what they had with Sam. She loved Sam. She needed to tell Sam she loved him.

Dad commandeered the phone. "Has the Logan article situation calmed down in Gilead?"

"Thankfully, yes." Miley didn't count. She had an agenda that wouldn't be derailed. "Logan was impressed by our lawyer."

Dad nodded. "I'm glad it's sorted. I worry about you."

"I know, Dad. I learned a hard lesson from the Jarrod situation, and I'm not rushing into anything."

"I trust your judgment, and I hope Sam can visit Australia. I'm too swamped to take time off to travel to the States."

"We'll work it out, Dad."

Becky loved her family, and loved how supportive they were of her relationship with Sam. A joyful Easter Sunday was her plan. *He is risen.* She looked forward to the Easter service this morning with Sam and her Gilead church family.

ON SUNDAY AFTERNOON, Sam chatted with his friends at the cast and crew party held at Bed of Greens Truck Farm. His arm was around Becky's waist, and it felt right to have her by his side. They were good together. After the party, they'd drive to the ranch and celebrate Easter with his family.

Sam had been in high school when he'd first volunteered for the play. So much had changed in seven years. His annual involvement with the passion play had strengthened his faith. He'd miss hanging out with the cast and crew next year.

Connor had become a Christian while playing the Jesus role. Sam was glad he'd been at church this morning to witness Connor's baptism. Sam prayed that Connor's faith would continue to mature and grow strong roots. He looked happy with Zoey and her adorable little girl.

Letty's beaming smile, mostly in Dawson's direction, had surprised Sam. Letty and Dawson had managed to get to know each other and avoid Mrs. Alleghany's gossip radar at Heavenly Brew. Not an easy feat to accomplish.

Logan Miles had snagged the town gossip spotlight. He'd already left Gilead for sunny California. Logan's people were issuing a press release tomorrow on how Logan's role in the passion play had impacted his faith journey. Sam would keep on praying for Logan, and pray Logan would stand firm in the face of inevitable media storms.

Becky glanced at her phone and whispered near his ear. "We should get moving."

"Yup." Sam did a round of farewells with Becky. He was non-committal in his comments when people mentioned next year. Who knew what next year would bring?

In January, when Cindy had proposed the blind date idea, Sam had never expected that a blind date could lead to something more. His relationship with Becky would face challenges. He prayed they'd have a constructive conversation during their drive to the ranch.

At the wedding reception, he'd realized that it wasn't the logistics of a long-distance relationship that had broken his relationship with Miley. Absence hadn't made his heart grow fonder. If Miley had stayed in Gilead, he'd have worked out sooner that she wasn't the one for him. Miley still behaved like the immature sixteen-year-old he'd started dating all those years ago.

He left the party with Becky, and a long stretch of highway lay ahead. Miles of corn fields surrounded them. This was Kansas. He'd miss Kansas when he made the permanent move to Colorado.

Becky turned in her seat. "I'm ready to talk about Jarrod."

"Okay." He kept his eyes on the road. Settled back in his seat. They had hours to talk, including a small detour via his favorite diner. A chocolate shake would hit the spot.

"My sister, Kelly, introduced me to Jarrod."

"She's the sister who's in Japan."

"That's her. Kelly is very different to Mel. Kelly likes to party, and that's where I met Jarrod."

"Did you party a lot?" The question had to be asked.

"Not really. Partying with drunk people who like being high isn't my thing. I'm anti-drugs and not into drinking."

Sam nodded. He hadn't seen Becky drink alcohol since they'd met, and he agreed with her anti-drugs stance.

"Jarrod was charming and good looking. He's a well-known actor in Australia who'd failed to break into Hollywood."

"Is Hollywood where Jarrod met Logan?"

"Yes. They'd partied in L.A. and Jarrod had picked up a supporting role in Logan's movie that was filmed in Australia."

That made sense. "I'm guessing Jarrod introduced you to Logan."

"He did. Jarrod was on his best behavior around me. He went to my church and said all the right things. Jarrod had said he respected my views on not being intimate outside of marriage, and he never pushed the issue." She sighed. "He had me fooled."

His grip tightened on the steering wheel. "What went wrong?"

"Everything. It all started to unravel in January last year. We visited Byron Bay and stayed with Logan in his beach house, not far from town."

"Sounds nice." That explained the Byron Bay photos.

"The house was amazing, with a pool as well as the beach nearby. It was summer and the paparazzi were out in force."

"I don't know how Logan puts up with all those photographers in his face."

"It's not fun. You know the photos in the article? Jarrod cut himself out of them."

Sam gritted his teeth, hoping he'd never meet Jarrod in person. "There were three of you in the photos."

"Four of us in the Byron Bay photos. Logan was with a bikini model and wannabe influencer who was desperate for paparazzi attention."

He shook his head. "This Jarrod person isn't a good guy."

"He's an opportunist. At the beach house, the three of them were snorting white powder."

His jaw fell open. "Did you know Jarrod was using drugs?"

"Nope. I saw a different side of Jarrod in Byron Bay. A side I didn't like."

"Did they pressure you to take drugs?"

"Not at all. Jarrod was too stingy to pay. The street price is expensive, and he used Logan's supply. You'll hear Logan's rehab story soon."

He nodded. According to Cindy, Logan had been linked to the Hollywood party scene. Cindy suspected Logan had been to rehab, and that's where he'd become a believer. John Johnson was Logan's Hollywood connection to Gilead and the passion play.

"After the Byron Bay holiday, I started to question if Jarrod was on the level. He's an actor, and he made up stories to cover his tracks. He tried to convince me that he'd only used drugs with Logan to keep him as a friend and important business contact."

"Did Jarrod succeed in convincing you?"

"For a while." She wrung her hands together in her lap. "I was stubborn and didn't want to admit I'd made a mistake. Mel had disliked Jarrod from the start."

"Mel is smart."

"She's a good judge of character, and she'd also heard rumors that Jarrod was cheating."

Oh no. Poor Becky. "Let me get this straight. He was happy to not sleep with you because he was sleeping with someone else."

"Exactly. It was a media story, with photo evidence, that exposed Jarrod's affair with a married woman."

What a lowlife. He was glad Becky had escaped Jarrod's clutches. "Were you still in a relationship with Jarrod when the story broke?"

"I was. I broke up with him. He wasn't happy."

"Did Jarrod make your life difficult?"

"Unfortunately, yes. I got caught up in the media frenzy. Jarrod told lies about me and our relationship."

His frown deepened. "I'm sorry you had to deal with that."

"It wasn't fun. The worst part was the intrusion into my privacy. That's why I kept Logan's secret."

"Okay. I'm starting to understand why you're friends with Logan." Becky had dealt with prying reporters and photographers following her. No wonder she'd tried to hide her meetings with Logan in Gilead.

"Logan understood why I'd split from Jarrod and run away to Kansas. We talked about the Bible and our faith journeys. He's like a big brother."

Sam smiled. "I'm glad you could support each other."

"I'm glad you understand." She paused. "I was worried you'd dump me when you heard about the Jarrod mess."

He shook his head. "You've met Miley. I ignored all the warning signs and stayed in a dying relationship."

"Hindsight is everything. I'm still living with the consequences of my impulsive decision to date Jarrod and get caught up in his world."

"Jarrod and Miley are in the past. They can't hurt us."

"True. I've learned valuable lessons, and I want to focus on today. Not worry about the future."

Today was a good day. He is risen. Jesus had paid the price for his sins on the cross and conquered death. He'd forgiven Sam and wiped the slate clean.

Sam had forgiven Miley and let go of the hurt and betrayal. His conversation with Miley yesterday had given him closure.

They stopped at the diner to break the trip and arrived at the ranch after the sun had set. The sky had shown off in true Colorado style, providing a kaleidoscope of colors as they drove through ranch country.

The family gathered indoors, the aroma of sizzling beef wafting inside from the veranda. Uncle Joe manned the outdoor grill. His cousins were finishing up a board game at the dining table. Becky had joined Cindy at the table. Aunt Lori and Mom were in the kitchen, preparing salads.

Dad walked indoors, a big smile lighting up his face. A rare occurrence, and unheard of during past visits to the ranch.

Mom moved to his side. "Can we chat for a few minutes before dinner?"

"Sure." Sam walked with his mother along the hall to the library.

Mom closed the door. "Thank you for praying. God answered our prayers."

He smiled. "Dad looks happy."

She nodded, wiping tears from her eyes. "We had a breakthrough this morning. After church. Your father has shared that his ranch issue is related to the house."

"In what way?"

"He finds it confronting being inside the house. All the memories from after the accident."

"I'm sad it still bothers him." Dad's workplace accident had happened more than fifteen years ago. Sam had been too young to understand the severity of Dad's anxiety and depression. The physical wounds had healed, but the emotional distress had remained.

"It's an anxiety trigger. He's open to the idea of retiring here if we build a new house. We hope to have a bit of money left over for travel."

Sam nodded. "We could discuss building a house together."

"I wouldn't want to intrude on your life."

"It could be two separate houses under one roof connected with a common wall and lockable internal door. If I'm traveling and away for long periods, you and Dad could look after the house for me."

Mom's eyes lit up. "Are you planning a trip to Australia?"

"Maybe. I'll talk to you and Dad later, after we work out the details."

Mom hugged him tight. "I'm so happy for you. I was praying you'd find a way to make your relationship with Becky work."

"God has answered our prayers." Sam was thankful his parents were making progress on repairing their marriage. He'd talk with Becky after dinner and discuss their future plans.

~

AFTER DINNER ON EASTER SUNDAY, Becky ran her fingers along the spines of the old books lining the library shelves. Antique book smell was her jam. She'd noted the history books on the shelves during her previous ranch visit and planned on browsing the contents of a few books while visiting for spring break.

Sam appeared beside her and draped his arm around her shoulders. He dropped a kiss on her cheek. "We need to talk."

"Yeah, but I'd like to read. This book collection is amazing."

"It was my grandfather's. He collected old books."

She met his gaze. "Was he a scholar as well as a rancher?"

"His father, my great grandfather, was a professor. One day I'll tell you the story about how my great grandparents came to settle here."

"Four generations of cowboys. Impressive."

"Yes, ma'am."

She chuckled. "I'm not old enough to be ma'amed."

"I'd like to know you when you are. We need to talk about the future." He led her to the sofa and sat beside her. "What do you want to do with your life?"

"I honestly don't know." She cuddled closer to Sam. "A year ago, my life was in chaos. I thought a year away from Australia would help me work out what I wanted to do."

"Has it?"

"Sort of. I was lost when I arrived in Gilead. My therapist has helped, but I don't know. I didn't plan on meeting you."

He chuckled. "That makes two of us. But there's something I do know."

"What's that?"

He cupped her face, his gaze intent. "I love you, Becky Montford. I want our relationship to work."

Her heart swelled and overflowed with love. He loved her. She loved him. "I love you, Sam Williams."

Becky lifted her head and met his lips, their sweet kiss full of promise and hope for a future together. She wound her arms around his shoulders, loving the tender way he showed her how much he loved her.

She rested her head against his chest, content to stay within his embrace and listen to his heartbeat.

He pulled back and looked deep into her eyes, his gaze steady. "I'm open to discussing different options."

"Are you willing to visit Australia?" She hoped and prayed he'd provide the answer she wanted to hear.

"Of course." He squeezed her hand. "My first trip outside North America."

"That's exciting. Traveling is fun, and I need to go home in June."

He nodded. "I'm curious to meet your family and see the places where you grew up."

"We can video call with Mum tonight." She pulled her phone out of her pocket and shot Mum a short message. "It's Monday morning in Australia."

"I don't know how you keep the time zones straight."

She waved her phone. "I have an app and use calendar reminders."

"Good idea."

"Dad would like to meet you. That will need to happen in Australia."

"Why's that? He doesn't travel."

She shook her head. "His hospital job is too busy. When do you think you could visit me in Australia?"

"Not until later in the year."

"What have you got lined up?"

"Selling my Gilead house and moving here. Summer at the ranch is busy and also a busy time for farm mechanic work."

"Can you continue doing farm mechanic work in Colorado?"

"Maybe. My employer might arrange a transfer, if there's work available."

"That sounds like a good option."

"Yes and no. I'd like flexibility to work on the ranch as well."

"Can you work for yourself? Set up a business." That could give Sam the best of both worlds.

"It's a possibility. I'd have to research and see if it's viable."

"Is visiting Australia in September or October an option?

"I think so. It's quieter from October, and my house should be sold by then."

She held his hands and stared into his beautiful eyes. "We can make a long-distance relationship work." She prayed they'd make wise decisions and seek His will as they made plans for a future together.

CHAPTER 16

*S*ix *months later*
    Sydney, Australia.

Sam lounged back in a deck chair at Becky's parents' waterfront home as the waves rolled onto the golden sand at Manly Beach. He adjusted his sunglasses and the rim of his new Akubra hat, Becky's gift to him when he'd landed at Sydney Airport four days earlier. Sam preferred his cowboy hat, but he'd indulge Becky by wearing the Aussie equivalent during his Australian visit.

Becky appeared on the spacious balcony, dropped a kiss on his lips, and handed him a coffee mug.

"Thanks." He smiled and inhaled the strong and aromatic brew, glad he was seated in the shade. Sunlight sparkled on the water like glittering diamonds.

"No problem." She settled beside him, coffee mug between her hands and sunglasses hiding her eyes. "Mum's making breakfast soon. Oatmeal the way you like it, plus bacon and eggs."

"Sounds good." Becky's mum was delightful, and she'd spoiled him with delicious meals. Australian bacon was like Canadian bacon, and leaner than the streaky bacon from home. He'd loved discovering Australian beef, and he was surprised when he'd liked the grilled Barramundi fish filets served at their family dinner last night.

Becky placed her Bible on the table between them. "We can do our Bible reading before breakfast."

"Definitely. I'll be more awake soon." He sipped his cappuccino, appreciating the double shot caffeine hit as his body clock struggled with the time zone adjustment. Surfers were on their boards, waiting their turn to ride a wave into shore. To the north, the headlands that separated the beaches were visible in the morning sunlight.

He understood why Becky had missed being near hills in Kansas. The suburban Sydney coastal region known as the northern beaches was covered in hills. They'd explored Sydney Harbour via the ferries, and Zach had invited them to go sailing on his yacht. Another new experience to cross off Sam's bucket list.

The day after his arrival. he'd spoken with Becky's father and asked permission to marry Becky. Sam had been intimidated by Becky's dad's high-flying medical career and was relieved to find her father approachable and supportive. Becky had a close-knit family, and they'd all welcomed him into the fold. Sam could envisage spending more time in Australia and exploring the countryside outside the Sydney city limits.

Becky's cosmopolitan lifestyle in Sydney was worlds away from Kansas and Colorado. Sam was thankful she was open-minded about where they could potentially live. He'd need to seek further qualifications in a mechanical specialty if they decided to live in the city.

Sam's Gilead house had sold during summer, and he'd picked up a new farm mechanic job based in Colorado. Mom was scheduled to retire next year. Sam had started building his ranch house, and Dad had agreed to the shared home arrangement that included a separate wing for Sam's parents.

Becky pointed at the ocean. "If we're lucky, we might see dolphins and whales."

"Really? That would be amazing." Being landlocked in middle America, he hadn't seen a lot of marine life in the wild so this was a whole new experience. Visiting the zoo and aquarium was on their Sydney must-see list.

Mel had taken him on an engagement ring shopping adventure. Becky had insisted she wanted the ring to be a surprise. The ring should be ready for Sam to collect from a family-owned jewelry store tomorrow. Sam had thought the mall he'd visited in Wichita was huge. The mall Mel had chosen in suburban Sydney had seemed like a mini city.

Becky placed her mug on the table. "Our plan for today is a walk around the Sydney Harbour foreshores."

"Sounds great. Where do we start?"

"Manly Wharf. We'll walk through Fairlight and around to Balgowlah. If we have the energy, we can continue on past Clontarf and finish up at the Spit Bridge in Seaforth."

"Okay." It was an easy walk to Manly Wharf from Becky's home. The other place names were unfamiliar, except for Balgowlah. Sam had appreciated Mel's tour guide assistance, and her helpful local knowledge in finding the right location to pop the big question.

He picked up the Bible. "What are we reading today?"

Becky reached for his hand. "Let's pray and continue reading in Jonah."

"That works." An appropriate book to study while sitting by the ocean. Sam closed his eyes, thankful that his love and relationship with Becky had grown during their months apart. He looked forward to discovering their future together.

~

A FEW DAYS LATER, Becky tightened her grip on the kite handle and propelled her kite higher in the strong wind. She jogged in the park overlooking Sydney Harbour, her ponytail flying around behind her. The sun on her face and the salty sea breeze was invigorating and refreshing.

Sam directed his kite inland and gave her a thumbs-up. The wind was too gusty to wear a hat or carry on a conversation without yelling.

It was years since she'd flown a kite at Dobroyd Head. When she was in high school, she'd played field hockey on the oval near the playground. The bushland in the surrounding national park provided spectacular views across the harbor toward Manly.

Two ferries crossed paths in the choppy water, the boats rocking and rolling as they passed through the open sea between North Head and South Head. The Tasman Sea lay beyond the coastline, a sizable chunk of the south-western Pacific Ocean that connected the east coast of Australia with the west coast of North America.

Becky had returned to her old job as a tour guide in Sydney. She was happy that Sam had arrived after the hectic October school holidays. She'd taken four weeks leave from work to spend more time with Sam in Australia, and an additional four weeks for her trip with Mum and Sam back to the States. Sam's family had invited her parents to visit their Colorado ranch. Dad would visit for a week in November, and fly home with her and Mum.

She hadn't made firm plans with Sam regarding their Australian itinerary. She'd promised Sam a horse riding adventure somewhere. In the States, they'd planned a road trip to the Rockies via Denver and Colorado Springs. They'd celebrate Thanksgiving at the ranch.

Sam pulled in his kite, gliding it into a graceful landing on the playing field. She crash-landed her kite on the grass.

Sam laughed. "I think you need more practice."

She poked out her tongue. "I told you I hadn't flown a kite in ages."

He gathered the kites and they walked together to Mum's SUV. Becky beeped it open, and they stowed the kites on the back seat. She was the designated driver, and Sam had to cope with being in the passenger seat. He wasn't complaining, now he understood her wrong-side-of-the-road confusion.

He pulled her into his arms and kissed her. She snuggled closer, having missed his kisses during their months apart.

He tipped up her chin. "Let's go for a walk to the lookout."

"Why? I'm happy to stay here and kiss you."

"We can kiss anywhere." He tugged on her hand. "I want to see the lookout."

"Okay." She chuckled and wrapped her arm around his waist. A signpost directed them to the path.

They reached the lookout and she cupped his face in her hands. "I'd rather kiss you than stare at the view."

He grinned and unzipped his jacket. Plucked a small jewelry box out of a pocket in the inner jacket lining.

Becky squealed. "Sam. Is that a ring?"

Sam dropped on one knee and looked up, his blond curls ruffled from the breeze. He opened the box. A diamond solitaire in a yellow gold setting sparkled in the sunlight.

She placed her hand over her heart. The ring was exquisite. It was happening. He was proposing. Here. Now. She wore no makeup, only sunscreen, and her hair was a windblown mess.

He held her hands, held her gaze, and captured her heart.

"Becky Montford. I love you, and I'd love to spend the rest of my days with you. Will you marry me?"

Her heart lifted higher and expanded wider than the magnificent kites they'd flown. "Yes. Yes. I love you, Sam Williams."

He slid the ring on her finger and over her knuckle. A perfect fit. He stood on both feet, lowered his head, and kissed her.

She stood on tiptoes and ran her fingers through his curls.

Warm tingles thrilled her. His arm circled her waist, holding her close. She loved this man and couldn't wait to marry him.

They came up for air, and she wrapped her arms around his back, resting her cheek on his chest.

"Top marks for surprising me." She closed her eyes, savoring the moment. "How did you make this happen?"

"Mel." He smoothed loose strands of hair off her face. "We went shopping when you were busy with your mother."

She loved Mel. "My sister is sneaky. Does my family know about this?"

He tipped up her chin and stared into her eyes. "They're planning a family celebration tonight, and an engagement party before we fly to the States."

"Let me guess." She could drown in the depths of his warm gaze. Full of love. Full of hope. "We'll have a second engagement party in Colorado."

"Yup. Our mothers have been talking."

She laughed. "That's dangerous."

"Always." His gaze lowered to her lips. "One more kiss and then we do photos."

Becky melted into Sam's embrace, forgetting about photos and family obligations. She wanted every detail from this moment ingrained as a treasured memory. They were blessed.

CHAPTER 17

*S*even months later
Colorado, USA.

Becky stood opposite Sam on the dance floor in the middle of a barn. The same spot where she'd first thought, during her January visit to the ranch last year, that the barn would be a fun location for a party.

Her first barn party had been their engagement party celebration six months earlier. Today they were celebrating their wedding. The traditional bridal waltz was done, and her feet had survived Sam. Cowboy boots helped, and the serious business of line dancing had commenced.

She'd been awake at dawn, too excited to sleep any longer. They'd exchanged vows at Sam's church in town and celebrated their wedding reception with family and friends at the ranch.

Becky had changed out of her delicate ivory wedding gown and wore a more practical white sleeveless dress. The shorter hemline skimmed the top of her matching cowboy boots. A dress designed for barn dancing, and horse riding from the barn to Sam's newly built ranch house for their first night together in their new home as husband and wife.

Sam held her hands and snuck a kiss. "Are you ready?"

"Bring it on." Line dancing was her new favorite form of exercise.

Her bridesmaids — Mel, Kelly, and Cindy — had also swapped their heels for cowboy boots. They'd learned all the dance moves last weekend at the wedding rehearsal dinner with Pete and Cindy's older brothers.

Her parents and Sam's parents were on the dance floor, keeping up with their offspring. Familiar faces formed a circle around them. Sam's Uncle Joe and Aunt Lori. Zach and Billie. Family who'd traveled to Colorado. Sam's friends from Gilead, including Pete and Emma, who wore a loose-fitting dress over her growing baby bump. Becky's friends from college. Their mutual friends from the passion play.

Logan Miles was there without a plus-one, and his presence had sent many a female heart aflutter. Logan's gaze was again drawn to Mel. Becky would ask her sister about Logan later.

Sam pulled her out of the line and drew her close. "Are you happy?"

She nodded. "Today has been the best day of my life. Better than I'd imagined." Their guests moved into lines on the dance floor.

He snuck another kiss and led her back into the line. "Our honeymoon will be special."

"I can't wait." They'd spend two nights at the ranch before flying to Washington state with Zach and Billie. Their Aussie friend Joel was marrying Hannah in Trinity Lakes. Next stop was ten days in Hawaii, followed by three weeks in Australia, including their Aussie wedding celebrations.

Her problems in Australia had sent her running to Gilead. The passion play had drawn them together. She was blessed that her cowboy blind date had become her husband who she loved and cherished. They were blessed to have a love centered on

Jesus. A three-stranded cord that was strong enough to last a lifetime.

ABOUT EASTER IN GILEAD

I hope you've enjoyed visiting Gilead in my story. If you're new to the *Easter in Gilead* series, please check out the other Easter-themed books set in Gilead, Kansas by my talented author friends. The stories are connected via an annual passion play and have simultaneous timelines in the lead up to Easter. They can be read in any order.

Her Unlikely Hero (Connor Hamelin and Zoey Matthews's story) is by Valerie Comer.

Her Billionaire Benefactor (Wendy Hall and Preston Swift's story) is by Elizabeth Maddrey.

His Runaway Crush (Letty Stanton and Dawson Bauer's story) is by Heather Gray.

AUTHOR'S NOTE

Thank you for reading *Her Cowboy Blind Date*. I hope you enjoyed Bek (aka. Becky) and Sam's romance story.

Her Cowboy Blind Date is part of the *Easter in Gilead* multi-author contemporary Christian romance series. I was excited to have the opportunity to work with a wonderful group of authors friends in the fictional Gilead story world. The books in the series are connected by the setting and characters who crossover between stories.

Please consider writing a review and sharing your thoughts on my book with other readers. I appreciate every review I receive for my stories. Reader reviews can help other readers find books that they'll enjoy reading.

ACKNOWLEDGMENTS

For my husband and young adult children who provided the support I needed to finish this book. I appreciate all your love and patience as we overcame the obstacles and challenges along the road to publishing this book.

A big thank you to Valerie Comer, Elizabeth Maddrey, Heather Gray, and Deb Kastner for inviting me to join your Easter-themed group project. I've loved writing in our shared Gilead story world.

Thank you to Jen Richards for your insightful input on my first draft. I appreciate my family and friends, and my newsletter reader friends, who have provided prayers and support. To God be the glory.

Many thanks to my editor, Iola Goulton.

ABOUT THE AUTHOR

A fun loving Aussie girl at heart, Narelle Atkins was born and raised on the beautiful northern beaches in Sydney, Australia. She has settled in Canberra with her husband and children. A lifelong romance reader, she found the perfect genre to write when she discovered inspirational romance. Narelle's contemporary stories of faith and romance are set in Australia and international locations. To find out more visit her at Narelle-Atkins.com

Narelle also invites you to join her author newsletter list. Her newsletter subscribers are the first readers to see cover reveals and hear bookish news from Narelle.

OTHER TITLES BY NARELLE ATKINS

Sydney Sweethearts Series

Book 1 - Her Tycoon Hero

Book 2 - Winning Julia's Heart

(previously titled Winning Over the Heiress)

Book 3 - Seaside Proposal

Book 3.5 - Seaside Christmas novella

(previously in *An Aussie Summer Christmas* box set)

Trinity Lakes Romance Series

Never Find Another You

A Tuscan Legacy Series

Solo Tu: Only You (A Tuscan Legacy, Book 7)

Sapphire Bay Series

His Perfect Catch (novella)

(previously in *SPLASH!* box set)

A standalone novella and spinoff story from *Seaside Proposal* set in
Sapphire Bay.

www.ingramcontent.com/pod-product-compliance
Lightning Source LLC
Chambersburg PA
CBHW020810190726
48285CB00006B/2234